One Hot DEAL

Other Books by Anna Durand

One Hot DEAL

Hot Brits, Book Eight

ANNA DURAND

JACOBSVILLE BOOKS · MARIETTA, OHIO

ONE HOT DEAL

ISBN: 978-1-958144-02-2 (paperback)
ISBN: 978-1-958144-03-9 (ebook)
ISBN: 978-1-958144-04-6 (audiobook)

Manufactured in the United States.

Jacobsville Books
www.JacobsvilleBooks.com

Publisher's Cataloging-in-Publication Data
provided by Five Rainbows Cataloging Services

Names: Durand, Anna.
Title: One hot deal / Anna Durand.
Description: Marietta, OH : Jacobsville Books, 2022. | Series: Hot Brits, bk. 8.
Identifiers: ISBN 978-1-958144-02-2 (paperback) | ISBN 978-1-958144-03-9 (ebook) | ISBN 978-1-958144-04-6 (audiobook)
Subjects: LCSH: Man-woman relationships--Fiction. | Bodyguards--Fiction. | Billionaires--Fiction. | Pregnancy--Fiction. | British--Fiction. | Americans--Fiction. | Romance fiction. | BISAC: FICTION / Romance / Contemporary. | FICTION / Romance / Romantic Comedy. | GSAFD: Love stories.
Classification: LCC PS3604.U724 O5441 2022 (print) | LCC PS3604.U724 (ebook) | DDC 813/.6--dc23.

Chapter One

Derek

I love my life, because I have the best job on earth—guarding the body of a beautiful, smart, powerful woman. Diana Sangster has built an empire by never giving up and never taking any guff from anyone. The woman is a billionaire, after all, which means she's way out of my league. Not that I've ever tried to make time with her. We've never shared more than mild flirtation, though I can't deny that I often have dirty dreams about her. Hey, I'm an unattached guy in a new country. What do you expect? Of course I dream about her. It doesn't mean I'll ever do anything about it.

But damn, those dreams...

I bump into Diana, and she glances back at me over her shoulder. Her brows lift, but her sunglasses hide her hazel eyes, so I can't tell if she's squinting at me the way she often does when people annoy her. I mumble an apology. She faces forward again and continues walking down the steps.

What an idiot I've become. Not watching where I'm going? That's unacceptable. I know better, but my fantasies about Diana distract me more and more every day. It's ridiculous. Never in all my career as a professional bodyguard have I gotten so distracted by a client that I screw up. *Snap out of it, man, and stop staring at Diana's ass.* I lift my gaze and go back to doing my job. I keep a hand lightly on

Diana's back as we walk down the steps, and I survey the area for any potential threats. In the three months I've been Diana's bodyguard, I haven't come across anything that even faintly resembles a threat. But she hired my company to protect her and specifically requested that I keep her safe.

Why? She claimed it's because she wants the "top man" to protect her, and I own the company. Diana said that five minutes after we met.

Diana and I reach the last step. Just as Ellie, my right-hand woman, reaches to open the door to the limo, a man pops out from behind a bush. He rushes toward Diana.

I thrust an arm out in front of Diana and push her behind me.

The man keeps coming.

"Stop right there," I snarl. Then I step fully in front of Diana, thrusting out an arm to stop the scruffy moron. It's times like this when I wish the Brits would let bodyguards carry firearms. I doubt this guy is a psycho, but I have to treat every potential threat as a serious one. So I tell the dweeb, "Don't come any closer."

When the guy finally notices my hard stare, he freezes, his eyes wide. He blinks several times swiftly. His focus lands on Diana, then swerves to me. "I, uh, just wanted to talk to Ms. Sangster."

He speaks with a British accent, but that's hardly unusual. We are in London, after all. I still haven't quite adjusted to living among Brits. I'd better get used to it, though. My sister is marrying a British viscount.

"Back off," I say in my toughest voice.

The scruffy guy shakes his head. "Please, I just want to talk —"

"No." I remove my sunglasses so I can glare at the guy. "Send her a letter or an email. That's the only way you'll ever get to communicate with Ms. Sangster."

Out of the corner of my eye, I can see one side of Diana's mouth has kicked up. She's turned her head slightly toward me.

"At least let me give her my CV," the scruffy guy says. "I'm a data analyst."

Diana looks at the man. "Sommerleigh Sweets does not have any openings for data analysts. But thank you for your interest in the company."

"You're a business incubator too, right? I just need a little help to start up my company." The guy moves half a step closer to

Diana, and I give him my patented scary look. He glances at me and winces, then swallows hard. "I'm sorry. This was a mistake."

The loser scurries off down the street.

Ellie opens the back door of the limousine for us. I offer Diana my hand to help her into the vehicle. She gives me that half-smirk again as she slides across the seat.

I climb in and stretch my arm across the top of the seat. My fingers barely reach Diana's shoulders, but I hadn't intended to touch her. Draping my arm across the seat is more like a reflex, not a come-on, and I know Diana understands that. I've gotten to know a lot of things about her—some personal, but mostly business related. I know she takes her coffee black and that she likes to go for evening walks along the river twice a week. But I don't know anything about her personal feelings or her past. She's an enigma in a sexy black business dress.

The car starts rolling down the road.

"How was the meeting?" I ask. "I couldn't hear a thing, even though I had my ear pressed to the door."

She takes off her sunglasses and turns slightly toward me. "Even if you had heard, you wouldn't have been able to tell anyone. You signed a nondisclosure agreement when I hired your company."

"I was joking, Diana."

"Yes, I know that." She eyes me up and down. "You were quite impressive when that silly man accosted me."

"Just doing my job."

She turns toward me even more and crosses her legs. Diana has the shapeliest legs I've ever seen. "Is that really your only concern?"

"What else is there? I am the job, that's why you hired me. I'm a workaholic, which means I can devote all my time to managing your protection detail."

"Hmm." She rests a hand on her knee and taps one finger on it. "You are strong and virile, healthy too. I know because I required you to have a physical before signing a contract with me."

What on earth is she getting at? If Diana thought I wasn't doing my job well enough, she would tell me outright. No beating around an invisible bush. She'd rip a branch off and whap me on the head with it.

My gaze wanders to her legs, and my dick jerks. *Stop looking, jackass.* I tear my focus away from her shapely calves and give myself a mental slap to the face.

Since I know Diana likes to get straight to the point, I give her the courtesy of doing the same. "Is something bothering you? If anyone on my team has done something you don't like, you know you can tell me. If I'm the one you're not happy with, the same applies."

"Oh, I'm very satisfied with the work you do, Mr. Hahn."

"Good. But there's clearly something on your mind."

She turns toward the front, gazing straight at the back of the driver's head. "Nothing urgent."

When Diana Sangster turns away, it means the conversation is over. Might as well let her shut it down, since I have no clue what she was trying to say.

Neither of us speaks again on the twenty-minute drive to her swanky flat along the River Thames. Ellie and Tim, our driver, wait while Diana and I get out of the car. I opened the door for her this time, and her lips curl into a full-on smirk. Tim and Ellie take the car into the parking garage while I escort Diana to the elevator, or as Brits call it, the lift. I kind of like that word. It saves a few syllables.

Once the lift doors close, Diana speaks. "I will be going for a walk this evening."

"You know, Geoffrey could escort you on the walk. Anybody could, actually." But I know she wants me and only me to accompany her. She always does. Once in a while, though, I like to prod her in the hopes she'll finally tell me why she insists on having me with her during those walks along the river.

"I don't want Geoffrey, or anyone else. You know that."

"Just checking. Thought you might like to switch things up for a change."

She moves only her eyes to glance at me sideways. "I do not switch things up."

Yeah, I know that about her too. Never hurts to try, though.

Once we walk into Diana's flat, she heads for the upstairs bedroom to change clothes. Since I have nothing else to do while I wait, I survey the flat. I've been here more times than I can count, and I know every inch of this place. It doesn't suit Diana. The spare, modern design seems more appropriate for an office space, not an apartment. This doesn't feel like a home. Diana might be tough as nails at work, but I've seen other sides of her since she hired me to protect her. Well, my company, that is. But I think it was really Hugh Parrish's recommendation that got me the job. He and Diana became business partners, and he's marrying my sister. So Diana got two recommendations.

Yeah, Avery tells everyone I'm amazing. It's kind of embarrassing.

Diana trots back down the stairs, now wearing designer sweats and a matching hoodie. She has designer sneakers too. When she goes for walks, she always pulls her brown hair back in a ponytail. I love that. It makes me want to kiss her. But I will never, never do that. I'm her bodyguard, not her lover.

Maybe I do sometimes fantasize about rolling around in the sheets with her. But it's only a fantasy. Just like my dreams. A woman of Diana's caliber would never get involved with a man like me.

Diana leads the way as we head out of her flat and exit the building, jogging across the street to the path that skirts the River Thames. She always likes to go for walks just as the sun is setting, then go back to the flat for a quiet dinner. I stay a discreet distance behind her as she ambles along the riverbank. As usual, she stops at one specific spot, though I can't see anything special about it. She gazes across the river, smiling slightly, and shuts her eyes for a moment.

God, she is so beautiful. And she seems younger this way too. I want to march over there, pull her into my arms, and just hold her.

Diana starts walking again.

And I follow. It's my job, that's all.

Our evening stroll takes forty-five minutes, out and back, then we're in the lift again, on our way up to Diana's flat. As the elevator doors shut, Diana glances at me sideways.

"Thank you for always wearing a suit," she says. "I appreciate the professionalism your team always shows."

"It's our job. And my team likes getting the chance to dress up. Most of our clients these days want their protection detail to blend into the background, which means wearing everyday casual clothing."

"Men look quite sexy in suits."

Did she just hit on me? She does do that sometimes, but I don't think she meant to flirt this time. Diana was stating an opinion that could apply to any man.

"I'd love to see you in a designer suit," she says. "Your physique would perfectly fit Armani's style."

"Thank you," I reply slowly, while I try to decide if she's really hitting on me this time. Not that I mind. But every time she says something like that, I fight the almost overpowering impulse to drag her into me for a hot kiss.

Diana doesn't say anything else once we exit the elevator and head into her flat. While she prepares dinner for herself, I wish her good night and leave. Then I have a solo meal in my own flat and watch an action movie I've seen five times before. By ten o'clock, I'm in bed, falling asleep.

I dream of Diana Sangster, naked, lying beneath me while I make love to her until we're both slicked with sweat and too exhausted to fuck anymore.

Damn, if only that fantasy would come true. But I'm her bodyguard, not her lover.

Chapter Two

Diana

I like knowing Derek Hahn is always watching over me, except when I'm at business meetings. Even then, though, I know he's in the hall waiting for me, ready to usher me out to the car and to wherever else I might need to go. Maybe part of the reason I like knowing that is because I enjoy looking at him. Though I've never seen him naked, I can imagine what he might look like. The man has powerful muscles, the outlines of which I can see quite well through his suit. I had never been attracted to a man at first sight until I met Derek. Now I can't stop thinking about him.

But the last thing I need is a man in my life.

Unless he's my bodyguard.

Three days have gone by since I told Derek he should wear Armani because he has the perfect body for that style. Can't believe I discussed clothing with him. But spending so much time with that man has turned me into a ruddy moron.

After precisely forty-five minutes of ambling along the river, we walk back to my building, with Derek following at a discreet distance as usual. Only when we enter the lift does he move to stand beside me.

"How was your walk?" Derek asks.

"Quite lovely. Did you enjoy it?"

"Oh yeah. The view was spectacular." He glances down at my arse. "The best I've ever seen."

The hairs at the nape of my neck tingle and stiffen as if he had exhaled a breath onto my skin. I experience a strong urge to grasp the lapels of his suit jacket, haul him into me, and kiss him. What would his lips feel like? What would he taste like? I will never know because I will never do the things I fantasize about.

I should tell him never to stare at my arse again, but it's too late for that. And besides, I don't want him to stop. If he did, I would need to stop admiring his arse.

As we enter my flat, Derek holds the door open for me. Once I've crossed the threshold, he moves to leave, grasping the knob as if to shut the door behind him.

"What are you doing?" I ask, half turning toward the door.

"Going home."

"I require twenty-four-hour protection. That is what our contract states."

Derek nods toward something past me. "That's why Ellie is here. And Geoffrey will be here in one hour, which means you'll have plenty of protection. Good night, Ms. Sangster."

Though I want to order him to stay here, that would be inappropriate. So I nod curtly and climb the stairs to my bedroom on the second floor. I'm halfway up the steps when I hear the front door click shut. My fingers grip the handrail more tightly. Derek has left.

No, that doesn't bother me at all.

I trudge up the stairs and pause to peer out the window, so I can watch Derek hailing a taxi. As the vehicle drives away, I hurry into my bedroom and change into my nightclothes. Just as I'm crawling into bed, my mobile rings. The screen tells me who's ringing me, and I rush to grab the mobile and say hello.

"Did I wake you up, Diana?"

"No, dear, you did not. I'm always awake at this hour." My attention swerves to the clock on the nightstand. "Why are you still awake? It's past your bedtime."

"I'm not a baby anymore. I'm fourteen, and I don't need a bedtime."

She says that in a long-suffering tone, as if I'm unbearably old-fashioned. Perhaps I am. And perhaps that's why Derek Hahn won't seduce me. He is nine years younger than I am, after all. Why should that stop me? And why haven't I tried to seduce him? We are both adults, and I haven't slept with anyone since long before I met him. I have never been afraid to go after what I want, whether it's a business deal or a man, so I can't understand why I'm hesitating with him. Well, his sister is marrying my business partner. But no, I can't possibly be afraid of what other people might think. I don't do that.

"Are you still there, Diana?"

I shake off my idiotic thoughts. "Yes, dear, I'm here. But honestly, Pippa, you should be asleep at this hour."

"And you should get married. If you had a baby, it wouldn't bother you so much that I'm away at school."

For a moment, I can't speak. Will I never get used to the way children blurt things out? But it's more than the way she said it that caught me off guard. It's what she suggested. Can the girl read my mind? No, of course not. Besides, this is hardly the first time she's commented that I need a husband. I do not need one of those, not ever again. But I have been contemplating a plan that meshes with what Pippa suggested. I can't tell her that, though. My idea is…radical.

"Are you away with the fairies again?" Pippa asks.

"No, of course not," I say, rather too sharply. "I'm sorry, pet. It's been a long day, and I need some rest. So do you. Even a mature fourteen-year-old shouldn't stay up this late."

"All right, all right. I'll go to bed if you will."

"It's a deal."

Silence follows, but I can hear her breathing. "Why did you send me away? Did I do something wrong?"

"No, love, of course not. I wanted you to have the best education available, and a boarding school seemed the most appropriate choice. You have friends there, don't you?"

"Yeah. But I want to come home."

A pang stabs into my chest, and my throat tightens. I miss Pippa more than I could ever tell her. "We can discuss that later. Good night, love."

"Good night, Diana."

After we've ended our call, I curl up under the covers and try to sleep. My thoughts keep returning to Derek Hahn. That dark hair. Those deep blue eyes. Those kissable lips. And that body. My word, that deliciously sexy body. How could any woman fall asleep while thinking about Derek? He's too young for me, but I only need one thing from him. A small donation. Hardly anything at all.

I drift into a semi-slumber, not completely asleep, but not really awake either. In this state, my mind conjures images of Derek Hahn naked. He crawls up my bed, under the covers, his nude body skating over my flesh. The sensual friction of his skin on mine spurs me to moan and writhe while I rub my hands over his back. His cock brushes against my mound, hot and hard and ready for anything I want him to do to me. The fantasy becomes so vivid that I swear I can feel his cock pushing inside me, filling me up until I can't breathe anymore. Heaven help me, I need him to fuck me in real life.

My lids fly open as a realization hits me. Oh, this will be even better than my original plan. A simple donation? Why should I settle for that? I can get everything I want with no strings attached. Assuming he agrees to my plan.

Have I gone barmy? Perhaps. But Pippa was half right. I don't need a husband, but I do want a baby. I've wanted it for some time now, wanted it more than I probably should. I'm forty-five years old, so this might be my last chance.

Yes, I will do it. Tomorrow.

Now that I've decided what I want and how I want it, I fall asleep quickly and don't wake again until morning. I feel more relaxed than I have in a long time, which might explain why I drift back to sleep before I've even pulled the covers off.

"Wake up, Diana."

Did someone speak? I must have imagined it. That voice sounded like Derek's, and that surely means I've fallen back asleep.

"Wake up, Diana," that stern yet sexy voice commands. "You'll be late for work if you don't get out of bed right now."

If I were awake, I wouldn't appreciate his tone. But in my lustful dreams, I love the way he's talking to me in that bossy tone. I mumble, "Why aren't you under the covers with me?"

"Excuse me?"

Now he sounds confused. Well, this is my dream. I can change his attitude anytime I want. "Tell me how you want me to suck you off."

Silence follows. The kind that doesn't seem appropriate in a dream. Derek clears his throat. That definitely does not seem like something I would imagine in a fantasy. But I must be asleep, mustn't I?

"Uh, Diana…what are you talking about?"

I spring up, shoving the covers off me, and stare wide-eyed at Derek. "What on earth are you doing in my bedroom, Mr. Hahn? It's highly inappropriate."

Standing there in a dark blue suit that tastefully highlights his physique, Derek lifts one brow and smirks. "I think you just offered to do something that's outside the requirements of our contract."

"What?" I swing my feet off the bed but trip and almost fall. I would have fallen, for sure, but he catches me. For a moment, I'm frozen with my body pressed to his and our gazes locked. Then I push away from him. "You could have used the intercom. It wasn't necessary to enter my bedroom."

"I tried the intercom. Guess you were so into whatever dream you were having that you didn't notice." He smirks again. "Now, would you like to tell me about that dream you were enjoying so much?"

Lifting my chin, I give him my haughtiest look. "I have no idea what you are talking about. But leave my bedroom this instant."

He salutes. "Yes, ma'am."

Derek pivots on his heels and saunters out the door, closing it behind him.

An hour later, I walk into my office at the international head-quarters of Sommerleigh Sweets. Derek had the courtesy not to mention my dream again, but I never expected he would mention it. Hugh will be in his office already, I'm sure. But I don't need to speak to him. I have only one meeting in mind for today, and it will be off the record. Derek Hahn doesn't even know I want to see him today, but he'll find out soon enough. First, though, I need to take care of a few business matters.

Once I've done that, I reach for my desk phone. My hand hovers over it, but I can't seem to make it respond to my mental command to grasp the handset. This is ridiculous. I am not anxious. I retract my hand, fist my fingers, and then snap them straight. Yes, I feel much better now. So I grasp the phone and dial the extension.

"What can I do for you, Ms. Sangster?"

Derek's deep, sensual voice makes my nipples tighten. Maybe there's a draft in my office. I sit up straighter, and for some reason tug my suit jacket down, though he can't see if my clothes are straight or unkempt.

"Are you still there?" he asks. "Or have you fallen asleep again?"

"Don't be ridiculous." I take a deep breath and exhale it slowly. "Please come to my office, Mr. Hahn. I need to speak with you in person."

"Sure thing. Just let me finish up this paperwork first. I'll be there in ten minutes."

"Excellent."

I hang up the phone and wait.

And I try not to think about his body. But commanding myself not to think about that only serves to increase my desire to fantasize about what might happen once I share my plan with Derek. I might have him inside me this morning, if I handle my proposal correctly. Will he take me on my desk? Oh, how I've fantasized about that over the past three months.

I straighten my jacket again—and wait.

Chapter Three

Derek

The boss lady has summoned me to her office. She likes to do that, but not usually to me. I've watched countless people trudge through her door, expecting to get fired or at least chastised. Hugh doesn't like dealing with stuff like that, but Diana takes it all in stride. That's what makes them a good team. Their strengths and weaknesses mesh perfectly.

I think Diana and I could mesh perfectly too, in a different way. The naked way. But I won't jeopardize my contract with Sommerleigh Sweets just to get laid. Other people are relying on me for their livelihoods.

Since I know Diana values punctuality, I knock on her office door precisely ten minutes after I spoke to her on the phone. She tells me to come in, and I shut the door after me, then take a seat in the chair across the desk from her. She has a huge desk. Five people could sit side by side behind that big mahogany monstrosity and still have room to spare. I don't understand why she has a huge desk, since Diana doesn't seem like the type to show off. Maybe it's an intimidation tactic. If so, it doesn't work on me.

I set one ankle on the other knee and relax into my chair. "So, what's up, Ms. Sangster?"

"This morning you called me Diana. And last night in the limo too."

"Oh. Ah, sorry. Sometimes I forget my manners."

"No, you never do that. I don't mind if you want to call me Diana." She rolls her chair closer to her desk, folding her arms on its surface. "I like it, actually. Everyone finds me intimidating—except for you."

"I've been a bodyguard for too long to let anybody get under my skin." Though I'd love to crawl under her skin. Or maybe just crawl under the covers with her. This morning, I swore she offered to suck me off, and I don't think that was a weird British saying. "What can I do for you this morning, Diana? I assume there was a reason you wanted to see me."

"There is indeed a reason." She fiddles with the papers on her desk, seeming almost nervous. But Diana does not get nervous. Finally, she clears her throat and looks straight at me. "I would like to discuss a personal matter with you."

"Okay. Shoot."

Diana just watches me for a moment. Then she leans back in her chair and shifts her hands to her lap. "It is a sort of business proposal, though it's personal business rather than company related."

Am I hallucinating, or is she delaying? Nah, it can't be that. This woman can deliver a speech to an audience of a thousand without batting an eyelash. I know that because I've escorted her to big conferences and stood at the back of the hall waiting for her to finish.

"What sort of personal business?" I ask. "Are you sick or something?"

"No, no, it's nothing like that."

I fidget in my chair. Now I'm suddenly feeling anxious. "Just tell me your proposal."

"Yes, of course." She studies her desktop. "This endeavor will require absolute secrecy and confidentiality. No one can ever know about our arrangement, if you should agree to it."

"Come on, you know you can trust me. I've been protecting your for three months."

She stares down at her lap while biting her lip.

That's the cutest thing I've ever seen her do, but it's damn strange too.

Finally, she sits up straighter, tugs her jacket down, and faces me. "I want to have a baby, but I do not need a husband or any sort of man in my life."

"Uh, okay." Where is this conversation going? Maybe she wants me to vet adoption agencies for her.

She clears her throat again. "I want you to be my donor."

"Your what? I don't have gazillions in the bank like you. Not sure how I can—"

"No, Mr. Hahn, not that sort of donation." She nails her gaze to mine. "I want you to be my sperm donor."

My eyes must be bulging because I can feel a draft drying them out. My mouth must have fallen open too. Yeah, my tongue is turning into a dry sponge in my mouth. I heard that wrong, right? She couldn't have said she wants me to donate my, uh, little guys.

"You seem confused, Mr. Hahn," she says. "Haven't you heard of sperm donation?"

I wince. "Could you please stop using the S-word?"

She sighs and shakes her head. "Why are men so sensitive about using the correct scientific term for their—"

"Because we are." The full meaning of what she said finally penetrates my brain. "Are you seriously asking me to go into the restroom and jerk off into a plastic cup?"

"I see crude terms don't bother you. But the word sp—"

"Yeah, you can stop saying that. I know what you're talking about."

"Good." She fiddles with the papers on her desk again. "You are healthy and virile, so I assume your sper—I assume you're healthy in other ways too. But I will require you to find a doctor and ask them to test your fertility."

"I haven't agreed to your cockamamie plan yet. And you haven't fully explained it." I scratch my head because it suddenly feels like I have fleas in my hair. "You said you don't want a man in your life, so I'm guessing you'll be taking my, uh, little guys to your doctor for, you know, the, uh, procedure."

Maybe I'm still asleep and this is one wacko dream.

"Privacy is of paramount importance to me," she says. "You know that. I cannot have anyone finding out what we are doing together. That means no doctors, not until I'm pregnant. No fertility clinics, no sperm banks, nothing that might leave a paper trail."

She said *that* word again, but I'm too confused to grimace about it.

I scrub a hand over my mouth. "But you said I need to see a doctor."

"Yes."

"What am I supposed to tell them? They'll want to know why I need a fertility test."

She gives me her businesswoman stare, which I've seen her give to a lot of people who work for her. It usually makes them apologize and vow never to disappoint the boss again. But Diana is not my boss, and she doesn't intimidate me.

"Tell them whatever you like," she says, her tone cool and calm, in opposition to the fire in her eyes. "Just get it done."

"Yes, ma'am. I'll do that—if I decide to accept your offer. But I still have some questions."

She waves her hand at me. "Go on."

"What happens after I get you knocked up? Am I supposed to just keep working for you and pretend we don't have a child together?"

Diana clasps her hands on her desk and studies me for a moment. "This will be my child. No one will ever know who the father is."

"Not seeing the incentive for me to do this. Abandon my own kid? That's not my style, Diana."

She gently bites the corner of her lip, and I swear I see a hint of vulnerability in her eyes. But she erases that quickly, reverting to her all-business attitude. "If you do this for me, I will compensate you handsomely. You might call it a promotion."

"I don't work for you, which means you can't give me a promotion."

"Of course I can, though not in the traditional manner." She leans back in her chair, aiming those beautiful eyes at me. "I can guarantee you a contract with an A-list celebrity who is in need of your services. The financial rewards will be great, and the contract will enhance your company's image far more than I could ever do."

"That's a generous offer. But I'd see our kid all the time and not be able to treat them as my child. Not sure I can pull that off. Hugh

Parrish works with you, and my sister Avery is marrying him. I'd still see a lot of you and our baby."

"I'm not finished. This new job will be in America." She waves a dismissive hand. "Problem solved."

For three months, I've protected this woman and gotten to know her a little bit, as much as she lets anyone know her. I've always had the feeling she had a relationship in her past that blew up in her face and now she's afraid to let anyone in. Maybe that's why she's doing this.

Or she might just be insane. But I can't believe that. Diana built a billion-dollar empire all on her own. She's amazing, not crazy. So why is she asking me to participate in her wacko scheme? Before I can give her any kind of response to her suggestion, I need to figure out a few things.

"I need time to think about it," I tell her. "You kind of blind-sided me, and I can't say yes or no yet."

"Of course." She nods and rises. "Thank you, Mr. Hahn."

"Uh-huh." I get up and start to walk away, then realize something. I turn toward her. "You never told me exactly how you plan for me to get you knocked up. If it involves a turkey baster—"

"Don't be ridiculous."

"Okay. How, then?"

Her lips twitch, like she's trying not to smile. "We will have sex, repeatedly, until I become pregnant."

I stare at Diana. I'm probably gaping at her, actually. Every muscle in my body refuses to work, even the ones in my eyelids. The only part of me that still functions is my dick. It jerked when she announced she wants to fuck me over and over until we hit the jackpot. Yeah, that idea turns me on. It's what happens afterward that makes me uneasy.

When I can finally speak, I manage only one word. "Oh."

She raises her brows. "Are you all right, Mr. Hahn?"

I blink several times rapidly, then clear my throat. "I'll think about your offer, Ms. Sangster."

"Thank you."

Diana sits back down at her desk and starts rifling through papers. But I think she's pretending to focus on work. I doubt she's as calm and collected about what she suggested as she wants me to think.

I head for my office and do my job, arranging schedules for my employees, handling paperwork, and checking in with my people in the field. My company works for a lot more clients than just Diana Sangster, but she and Hugh offered to let me have an office at the headquarters of Sommerleigh Sweets and use it for all my clients, not just their business.

Hugh will be my brother-in-law in next Saturday. If I take Diana's offer, I'll move back to America, far away from my sister. Avery is the only family I've got. Well, until she marries Hugh. Then I'll technically have a brother.

This is nuts. I can't be Diana's baby donor.

For the rest of the day, I obsess over work stuff to keep from thinking about Diana and her deal. But after work, I can't avoid that anymore. It's time to escort Diana back to her flat. Ellie opens the limo door for us, and I see Geoffrey in the driver's seat. I help Diana into the car and slide in beside her, keeping a discreet distance as always. Ellie shuts the door. She will follow us in another vehicle, bringing up the rear of our little motorcade.

I watch Diana as Geoffrey pulls the limo out onto the street. She pretends she doesn't notice me watching her, but I know she does. Diana is a savvy woman. That's why I can't understand the deal she proposed. I'd love to have kids, but becoming a donor who disappears before the baby is even born… No, I don't see any way I can agree to that.

Maybe I could change her mind. And do what? Marry her? We don't really know each other. I lost my parents years ago, and my only serious relationship fell apart in the most painful way. I shouldn't get this deeply involved with anyone, much less a complicated woman like Diana.

Will I accept her offer? I have no fucking idea.

Chapter Four

Diana

Derek escorts me up to my flat, but he leaves as soon as I walk inside. Though he usually stays only if I'm going for a walk, I can't blame him for wanting to get away from me right now, considering what I suggested this morning. He must think I've lost my mind, and perhaps I have. I never wanted a baby until recently. Until I met Derek Hahn. But no, that has nothing to do with my decision.

When I go to sleep, I experience steamy dreams of Derek yet again.

That also has no bearing on my decision.

I spend twenty-three minutes choosing which outfit to wear today, though I have never taken so long to do that before. It means nothing. I want to look good today because Hugh and I will be opening our new factory in Camden this afternoon, and of course, Avery will be there as well to support Hugh. The man once known as Lord Steamy and ridiculed for one indiscretion has become a successful and respected businessman once again. I'm proud of Hugh, for the way he picked himself up and got back to work. Together, we have done more than save Sommerleigh Sweets. We have turned it into an international success.

Hugh Parrish has become almost like a son to me, though I doubt I will ever tell him that. I'm not the effusive sort. Other people are more likely to call me a dragon lady or a robot.

When I head downstairs to the living room, I see Derek standing guard near the door to my flat. Geoffrey is on the balcony, and Ellie will be waiting for us in the limousine, I'm sure. They take turns driving. But Derek always rides with me in the backseat.

Though I invite Derek and Geoffrey to join me for breakfast, they both assure me they've already eaten. Derek won't even look at me today. He stares across the living room from his position at the door, and when I made my breakfast offer, he simply shook his head.

I shocked him with my proposition yesterday. I must have done. He's uncomfortable around me now, and he must think I'm a lunatic. But I want him to say yes. I want it badly. Why? I can't answer that question. It's not because I'm attracted to him, though I am. And it's not because I know he will keep the secret. If he rejects my offer, I will give up on the idea altogether.

But that also means nothing.

In the limousine, Derek does not sit beside me with his body turned slightly toward me and his arm on the seat's back, as he usually does. Today, he faces forward and rests his elbow on the window frame, bracing his chin on his raised hand while he stares out at the streets rushing past us.

And I experience a strange impulse to comfort him. But I restrain myself.

I can't resist watching him, though, with furtive glances that I hope he doesn't notice. He seems pensive, which is probably because of what I asked him to do for me. Perhaps I should have suggested we try dating instead, but I've been down that road too many times and been severely disappointed. I once wasted years on a man who only pretended to love and respect me, then tore my heart to shreds. The risk of another heartbreak is too high. That's why I decided a few years ago that I would never date again. The only prudent choice for having a baby is to convince Derek Hahn to become my donor.

No one will ever know.

Derek helps me out of the car, but he doesn't speak or look directly at me. Once we're inside the building, Derek, Ellie, and Geoffrey go to the security office to handle their daily duties at Sommerleigh Sweets. Derek does walk me to the door to my office, but he leaves immediately after that.

He's going to turn down my offer, isn't he? I wish he would go on and do that so I can get it over with. Waiting is torture.

In the afternoon, we all climb into the limousine for the trip to Camden, which will take half an hour, where we will officiate the grand opening of the new factory. Avery and Hugh try to engage Derek and me in conversation, but Avery winds up chatting to Hugh because we can't manage to speak to either of them, much less each other.

Hugh gives an excellent speech for the grand opening, then he and I cut a ribbon with an enormous pair of scissors. I hadn't wanted to do that since it's a silly tradition, but Hugh talked me into it. The man might not be Lord Steamy anymore, but he hasn't lost his ability to sweet talk anyone he chooses, male or female, old or young. If he ever met Pippa, she would develop an instant crush on Hugh. Teenage girls are very susceptible to his charms.

While Hugh chats to the employees, Avery snags my arm and leads me over to a secluded corner. "Are you okay, Diana? You seem kind of anxious today."

"Anxious? Good lord, no. I never feel that way."

She leans closer to whisper, "You can tell me, whatever it is. I won't say a word to Hugh about it."

It's not my business partner who has me feeling...on edge. "I am not anxious, dear, but I appreciate your concern."

"Okay, if you say so." I glance at the factory floor, where Hugh is charming the trousers off everyone he meets. Then movement just past Avery's shoulder catches my attention. "I think your brother wants to speak to you."

She glances back at Derek, who stands a short distance behind her.

Derek looks at me, then turns his head away and adjusts his tie.

Avery gives me a knowing smile. "So, how long have you been dating my brother? I don't mind. You two make a perfect couple."

Perfect? She's barmy.

I lift my brows at Avery. "You are mistaken, dear. I am not involved with Derek."

No, I only want him to be my donor. Perhaps I should consider the turkey baster idea that Derek mentioned. Then he could provide what I need without the necessity of having sex. That would be the cleanest, fastest way to get it done, though it might be somewhat tricky. Intercourse is the only surefire method for me to, um, receive his donation.

Bloody hell. Now I'm refusing to use the S-word.

Avery is still smiling at me as if she's positive she knows a brilliant secret.

Before she can interrogate me any further, Hugh approaches us. "The grand opening is over. We can all go home."

"That was quick," Avery says. "I assumed it would take hours, not thirty-five minutes."

Hugh shrugs. "Why waste time? Everyone wants to get things rolling."

"He's right," I say. "The grand opening was mostly for the media, so they would have photographs to print in their papers."

Derek and I follow Hugh and Avery out of the building and into the limousine. None of us speak. When we drop the happy couple off at their flat, the second the car door shuts, Derek turns partway toward me and lays his arm across the seat's back.

"Close the partition," he calls out to Ellie.

She doesn't hesitate, though I can see in the rearview mirror that she wrinkles her brows. The partition rises, giving us full privacy. Derek has never asked anyone to shut the partition before.

"We need to have a little talk, alone," he says. Then he slides closer to me, and his fingertips tease the back of my neck. "Tell me one thing, Diana. Are you doing this baby pact thing because you desperately want a kid? Or because you desperately want to fuck me?"

All the fine hairs on my body shiver and stiffen, but a sensuous heat rushes through me a second later. Between my thighs, the heat instigates a tingling sensation. I cannot want him simply because he asked an inappropriate question.

So I huff. "Don't flatter yourself, Mr. Hahn."

He stares at me with such intensity that a shiver slithers up my spine. The sensation isn't entirely unpleasant.

I stare right back at him.

Derek leans in until his lips graze my ear. "Before I decide whether to accept your deal, I need to gather a little more information."

"About what? I've told you how it will work."

"Yeah, but I need to know something else." He lays a hand on my thigh. "Whether or not we're sexually compatible."

"That doesn't matter. Men are easily aroused, and all I need is for you to reach orgasm."

"You don't care if either of us enjoys it."

The feel of his hand on my thigh, even with the barrier of my dress, excites me in ways I've never experienced with any other man. I don't understand it, and I don't like it. Well, I like it. That's obvious. I don't want to enjoy it, but his breaths teasing my ear… That's even harder to resist. My nipples have tightened and become so sensitive that I think I might come just from that sensation.

"Do you want me to move my hand?" he asks.

I shake my head just a little.

He slides his hand up to my hip. "The way I see it, if we're going to have sex over and over until we reach the finish line, we might as well enjoy it. I don't want to watch porn movies just so I can get it up for you. So let's make sure we're compatible—with a kiss."

I struggle to pull in a full breath, and my response emerges as a whisper. "All right."

"You want me to kiss you."

My head nods, but I had no conscious intention to do that. It's true, though. I want him to kiss me. I need it. Part of me prays it will be less than satisfying, so I can keep our arrangement clinical rather than sensual. But mostly, I want to know what it feels like to kiss Derek Hahn just once.

He cups my cheek in his hand, exerting gentle pressure to turn my head toward his face. The heat of his breaths makes my heart beat faster. As he leans in, my lids flutter shut and slick heat gathers between my thighs while my clitoris throbs. He hasn't even kissed me yet and already I'm on the verge of orgasm. The moment his lips touch mine, a breath rushes out of me as I sag into him.

Derek glides his hand up my cheek to tunnel his fingers into my hair. A deep groan resonates in his chest.

His lips feel soft and warm, and when he thrusts his tongue into my mouth, the velvety texture of it triggers a landslide of sensations that overwhelm me until I can't hold back anymore. I grasp his tie and drag him closer. With his chest mashed to mine, I push my tongue into his mouth and moan at how sinfully good he feels and tastes.

Keeping hold of his tie, I clutch his hand and thrust it between my thighs, under my dress, until his palm is spread over my mound. He pushes his palm inside my knickers, shoving his fingers between my folds, then pets my flesh so delicately that I can't catch my breath. My ears begin to ring while he strokes me with his long fingers, up and down, up and down, while my ears begin to ring.

We're about to shag, right here in the limo.

And I want it to happen.

Derek pulls his hand out of my knickers at the same instant that he tears his lips away from mine. "Damn, Diana, you're so fucking ready for me."

I can't speak. The intensity of his expression, of how much he wants me, takes my breath away.

He lifts his hand to his face, curls his fingers that glisten with my wetness, and sucks in a deep breath. His lips curl into a satisfied smile. "The scent of you drives me crazy."

My throat has gone thick, and my body still throbs from what we just did. I want more.

But he wipes his fingers on his trousers and shimmies backward across the seat. "I won't take you tonight."

He faces the front of the vehicle.

And I sag against the seat, still burning for him.

Chapter Five

Derek

I gaze down at the scrambled eggs on my plate, picking off bits of them with my fork just so I can move them around. But I'm not really paying attention to my food. I've eaten some of it, but I keep forgetting about the eggs because I can't stop thinking about Diana and her cockamamie plan. All night, I tossed and turned like a character in a bad movie, while trying not to imagine all the ways I'd love to try to give Diana that donation.

That kiss last night…it was incredible. But when she shoved my hand inside her panties, I almost blew my top.

So yeah, I woke up today with the hardest morning wood in history. It took me an hour in the shower to deal with the problem. No way did I want to show up at my sister's place in that condition. It's the weekend, and I always have breakfast with Avery and Hugh on Saturday.

"Are you listening, Derek?" Avery asks.

No, I wasn't paying any attention whatsoever to the conversation. I glance up and find Avery and Hugh both staring at me like I've been drooling onto my plate.

"Sorry," I say. "Uh, what were we talking about?"

"Your groomsman duties."

"Oh, that. Nobody really has groomsman duties, you know. It's not a thing."

My baby sister scowls at me. Like that will bother me.

"Callum is the best man," I say. "It's his job to deal with all the wedding garbage on the groom's side of things."

Hugh hikes up his brows. "Are you reneging on your promise to Avery?"

Oh, that's a dirty trick. He knows I would do anything for my sister, especially since our parents are gone. Having only each other made us very close. Hugh's dad passed away years ago too, so I'll be walking her down the aisle and also serving as a groomsman.

"Well?" Hugh says. "Are you going to disappoint her?"

"Of course not." I set down my fork and lean back in my chair, pinning my gaze to Avery. "How hard can it be? I stand at the altar beside Hugh and tackle Lord Sticky if he tries to make a run for it."

My sister narrows her gaze on me and tries to sound tough. "Don't harass Hugh. I love him."

"The guy used to call himself Lord Steamy. But you think it's terrible if I call him Lord Sticky?" I shake my head and make a sarcastically grave face, aimed at the Brit. "This marriage won't last unless you grow some backbone, Hugh."

"It's Lord Sommerleigh to you," the groom says. "Unless you'd care to amend your statement."

"Sure. I can think of lots of other things to call you, but I don't use that kind of language in front of a lady."

Avery rolls her eyes. "Are you two done cementing your bromance with stupid jokes?"

"Yes, darling," Hugh says. "Though I dispute the 'bromance' tag."

"Me too," I say. "We'll be bros-in-law soon, that's all."

Avery grins. "You guys finally agree on something. It's a miracle."

I finish up my eggs and bacon just so my sister won't fuss over me like I'm a toddler. I swear once she actually did the airplane thing to try to make me eat more—and that happened last year. Women are weird. Avery might drive me crazy sometimes, but I love her anyway. Even if she is marrying Lord Sticky.

But Diana drives me crazy in a different way.

The three of us collaborate to clean up after our meal, which results in plenty of sarcastic jibes, mostly between me and Hugh. He's a good guy, and I can't deny he makes my sister very happy. I never could've imagined Avery would hook up with a British aristocrat, but all I care about is her happiness. I'm looking forward to having a niece or nephew. I bet that will happen soon.

I've just walked out of the swanky building where Hugh and Avery live when my phone rings. I answer with my usual greeting, but I barely have a chance to do that before a familiar voice interrupts.

"There's been an incident," Diana says. "Nothing serious, but I thought I should let you know."

I freeze, and the couple coming up behind me almost stumble into me. They give me annoyed looks, but I'm focused on what Diana said. "What's wrong?"

"Wesley and Sheldon got food poisoning. They wanted to go out for breakfast and they both chose to eat Greek gyros from a dodgy street vendor. I bought croissants from a respectable cafe."

"Are the guys okay?"

"Yes. I took them to the nearest hospital, and the doctor assured us they'll be fine. But they won't be able to fulfill their duties today."

"I'll meet you at your flat. I can be there in twenty."

"Minutes?"

I stifle a chuckle. "Yes, Diana, minutes."

"But surely one of your other employees—"

"This is the weekend, and Geoffrey and Ellie need some downtime. I'll take over until Wes and Sheldon can resume their duties."

"But you need a weekend break too."

"Don't worry about me." I rush to the curb and wave at a taxi. As the driver pulls over, I yank the door open. "Relax, Diana. I'll be there soon."

"No, I'll be fine alone. Do not come here."

"Shut up, Diana. I'm coming."

I hang up and jump into the taxi, instructing the driver to take me to my flat first. I need to change clothes. Hugh "accidentally" spilled tea on my shirt. He offered to buy me a new shirt and a matching suit, one that would undoubtedly cost more than my college education, but I told him not to bother.

Does Diana not want me at her place because of our kiss last night? I think that must be the reason. If she can't handle a mind-blowing lip-lock, I don't get how she thinks she can manage to have sex with me repeatedly.

But I've got a plan. It came to me while Diana was trying to talk me out of going to her flat to take over protection duties. She sounded almost panicked when I informed her I would be there in twenty minutes. My place is only two miles away from Hugh and Avery's flat, and it only takes me a few minutes to change.

Since I paid the taxi driver to wait for me, I get on my way again quickly and reach Diana's flat on time, ringing the bell to let her know I'm here.

The door swings open. Diana blinks rapidly, then glances over her shoulder and looks at me. "It's been precisely twenty minutes. The clock on the cooker confirms it."

"A cooker is an oven, right?"

She nods.

"You know I'm always on time. If I say I'll be someplace in twenty minutes, that's when I show up."

Diana just stands there gaping at me. She's wearing a knit dress, kind of like a full-body sweater, and the fabric clings to every curve of her shapely figure. Am I surprised that she dressed up on Saturday? Nope. She does that a lot.

I take hold of her upper arm to gently urge her to back up so I can walk inside the flat and shut the door.

She still can't stop staring at me. "You're wearing a suit."

"Of course I am. I'm on duty."

"But you look..." She shakes off her shock and reverts to her usual stoic attitude. "You didn't need to be so formal."

Time to enact my plan.

I back her up to the entryway wall. "You like me in a suit. Said so yourself. I've seen the way you look at me and lick your lips when I'm dressed for work."

"Please. You are nothing more than an employee."

"Wrong. I don't work for you. We have a contract between our two businesses." I move even closer until my body brushes against hers. "After last night, you can't deny we have chemistry."

"That is irrelevant. And I don't need you here today."

I hook a finger under her chin and lift until our gazes meet. "It's my job to guard your body, Diana."

Her chest heaves, and seemingly without intending to do it, she traces her tongue over her lips. Yeah, she wants me. I want her too, but I realized early this morning that I can't be her baby donor and then walk away from my own child. I know Diana and I could have something together, but she's afraid to let anyone in. Maybe I have relationship baggage too, but I need to find out if Diana and I could have something together. To do that, I need her cooperation. I have a plan to show her what I believe she really wants and ease her into the rest.

I'm taking a big risk. She might panic and shut me out completely, but I have to try.

So I lower my head to within millimeters of her lips. "I'm accepting your deal."

Her eyes go wide, which makes her seem so innocent and sweet that I want to hold her. But I need to take this one step at a time.

She stares into my eyes while hers remain wide. "Why would you do that?"

"Because you asked me. I said yes, Diana, so you might want to thank me."

"I am…grateful for your participation."

Can't help chuckling. "Participation? That's cute."

She puckers her lips and squints at me.

I pin her to the wall with my body. "Let's get started on the baby-making right now."

Though her cheeks have turned pink, she tries to square her shoulders and give me a mulish look. But she only half succeeds. "No. We will do this on my timeline."

"Which is what? Next month? Might as well get going right now." I palm her breast. "I guarantee you'll love the way I knock you up."

"I don't appreciate your crude language." She takes hold of my hand and peels it away from her breast. "My timeline."

"Uh-uh. I'm the one doing all the work in this arrangement, so I get to set the pace. We start right here, right now."

"Not in the entryway."

"Okay. Where, then? The bedroom sounds good to me. A nice, soft mattress…"

She manages to straighten her spine at last and lifts her chin. "No bedrooms."

"How about the sofa? That would be hot too."

"I don't care if it's hot. Perhaps we should go back to your original idea—the turkey baster method. Then we wouldn't need to argue about where to do this."

Damn, she's sexy when she makes dumb-ass pronouncements. I hadn't been serious when I asked if that was how she planned on getting pregnant, but naturally, she latched on to it out of desperation. Yeah, she desperately wants to stop me from taking her in the bedroom or any comfortable, relaxed location. But I can adapt.

"I'm not arguing," I say. "I'm negotiating."

She squints at me again, with her lips puckered again.

That just makes me want to fuck her right here on the floor.

"No bedrooms or sofas," she tells me. "No armchairs either. Also, no hotel rooms."

"Okay." I glance around her sparsely furnished apartment. "That leaves us with the coffee table, the wood floor, the stairs, the kitchen, the walls, the picture windows, the bathroom—"

"No showers or tubs, either."

"Does that include hot tubs?"

"Yes."

She probably thinks her demands will make me give up and agree to the turkey baster concept. But no, nothing will stop me from finding one place we can both agree on where we can have sex.

"It's the coffee table, then," I say. "Strip, Diana."

She gives me her haughtiest look. "I will not do that. We keep our clothes on, except for my knickers."

I can't help chuckling again. "I'll need to at least unzip my pants."

"Yes, of course." She reaches under her dress and shimmies out of her panties, all without flashing me anything more than the barest glimpse of dark hairs. "I'm ready."

I unzip and pull out my dick, already hard and raring to go. But the thought that in a few seconds I'll be inside her... That makes my dick twitch and throb. Fuck, I want her.

Diana holds out her hand to me. "Let's shake hands to seal our agreement."

I clasp her palm. "It's a deal."

A damn hot one. Despite knowing just how many ways this could go pear-shaped, I won't back out now. She might have rules, but I've got a solid plan to prove to her I'm more than her bodyguard or her baby donor.

Why am I dead-set on winning her over? She's an amazing woman, but that's not the sole reason.

I've always loved trouble.

Chapter Six

Diana

Am I really going to do this? Here in my flat? I'd intended for our baby-making endeavors to be sequestered from my private and professional lives, but I hadn't yet figured out how to do that. I hadn't counted on Derek insisting on taking the place of his employees to guard me himself. He seems to have come here strictly to have sex. No, I can't believe he would do that. Derek is filling in for Wesley and Sheldon, just as he said, but he decided to take advantage of the fact we're alone.

The moment he walked into my flat, I started to get aroused. The more he talked about our arrangement, the more turned on I became. His voice always affects me, with his deep and rough tone, but that alone didn't do this to me. It's everything about him that drives me wild.

But I will not let my intense lust for him show. I must maintain control, even while we're shagging. Yes, that will be easy to do. I'm well-known for my self-control.

Derek strokes his cock, and his voice grows even deeper. "Sure you're ready for this, Diana? Once we fuck, our relationship will never be the same."

"Nothing will change, not for me."

He moves closer, our bodies inches apart, and slides one hand up my thigh to push the hem of my dress up to my hips. He licks his lips as he gazes at my groin, where the hairs on my mound have been exposed. I'm so wet that it's beginning to dribble down my inner thighs. He can't see that. My legs are too close together.

With a soft groan, he pushes his knees between my thighs and eases them apart. He can't notice the juices glistening on my skin. And surely he won't detect the scent.

"Damn," he says, his head bowed while he stares at my body. "You want me bad, don't you?"

"No more than any other man I've been with."

He flicks his gaze to mine. "Liar. I can see how much you want me." He drags his fingers up my inner thigh, then lifts them to his mouth—and sucks on them. An even deeper groan escapes his lips. "Mm, I'd love to feast on you for hours."

"That won't happen." I yank my dress up higher, exposing my hips and lower belly, then spread my legs even more. "Just get it done, would you? I have plans for the day."

"Yeah, I know." He smirks. "You've got plans to fuck me all day."

"Only once. Right now." I lash one leg around his hips, tugging him nearer until his cock brushes my belly. "Stop talking and just do it."

"Yes, ma'am." He grasps my hips. "Time for the baby-maker to do his job."

I know he's teasing me because he thinks my idea is insane, but he agreed to it. This shouldn't take more than a moment. Men reach orgasm far sooner than women do.

He pulls his hips back and slides his length inside me slowly. "Okay?"

"I've had sex before, many times, which means you don't need to treat me like a delicate flower." But the sensation of his cock gliding into me is making me breathe harder and tingle deep inside my body. "Stop dillydallying."

He smirks again and sighs. "Yes, Ms. Sangster."

Derek thrusts into my body hard and fast, making me gasp and arch my back. The fullness of him robs me of breath, and my fingernails scrape on the wall. What happened to doing this on the coffee table? I don't care where we do it, so the location doesn't matter.

He pumps into me with such vigor that my whole body bounces, and I can't squelch the sharp cries of surprise that burst out of me. I grow even wetter as he pins me to the wall and fucks me so hard that I have to clutch his shoulders to keep from falling down. Only the toes of my shoes touch the floor, and I mindlessly wrap both legs around his hips while he grunts and slaps one hand on the wall.

I clench my inner muscles around him.

"Gah, Diana," he snarls. "I can't—Ah!"

His entire body goes rigid, and I swear I can feel him coming inside me. He pounds his fist on the wall while he thrusts twice more, then sags against me.

"Shit," he mutters, while I remain pinned to the wall. "I didn't mean—Fuck, I wanted to make you come too."

Oh God, yes, I wanted that. I'd been on the edge right there at the end, but he went off before I could. It doesn't matter. I only needed him to provide the donation, and he's done that.

I set my feet on the floor.

Derek pulls out of me gradually and takes one step away from me. "That just won't do."

"What won't? You did your part. It's over until the next time I need a donation, assuming this time might not have done the trick." I still have my legs spread because I can't convince my muscles to obey my commands.

"That's not what I meant." He shoves his hand between my thighs to cup my privates. "I never leave a woman hanging. Never."

"I'm not that sensitive. This is hardly the first time a man has let me down."

A sly smile curves his lips. "Brits treat women that way? Let me prove to you American men are better."

"That's not necessary."

"Sure it is." He slips his fingers between my folds and begins to stroke my slick flesh. The orgasm I'd almost experienced a moment ago rises inside me yet again, and I'm suddenly struggling for breath. "Now that I've felt how much you want me, neither of us will ever forget it."

He presses his thumb into my clit and rubs, then lunges his head down to seize my nipple with his teeth, through my dress, and suck fiercely. With his fingers and his mouth tormenting me, I have no way to resist. Not that I want to, anyway. I need to come so desperately that I grasp his head and clutch it to my chest while rocking my hips into his touch.

My body freezes. My inner muscles begin to pulsate around his fingers, but instead of slowing down, he pumps his fingers faster and rubs my nub so vigorously that my heart pounds. The pleasure rockets through me, like a bolt of lightning that pierces my skin to electrify my every nerve. And I do something I have never done before, not in my entire life.

I scream.

He releases my nipple and possesses my mouth, ravishing me with rough strokes of his tongue. My orgasm rolls on and on, even while he slows the movements of his fingers, and the pleasure seems like it will never end. But finally, it fades away.

Derek steps back and wipes his fingers off on his shirt. "You are so fucking beautiful when you come."

The way he's looking at me… That doesn't seem like lust. It's much softer and sweeter. I do not want him to have tender feelings for me. That will cock up my plan. It will cock up everything. I need to keep my life in order.

Derek zips up his trousers. "Where should I stand?"

"Huh?" I still feel dazed by that climax, and I can't understand the words he just spoke. But my brain starts working again at last. "Oh. You mean to perform your bodyguard duties. Stand wherever you like."

"Yes, ma'am."

"Stop calling me that, please."

He straightens his tie. "Sure thing, Ms. Sangster."

The infernal man called me that just before we had sex. I don't think I'll be able to stand hearing him call me "Ms. Sangster" without remembering what we did. Of course, we'll be doing that again. And again. And again. However long it takes to accomplish the task.

Derek turns to walk toward the living room.

The doorbell rings.

We both freeze. He glances over his shoulder at me, and I swerve my gaze back and forth between him and the door.

The bell rings again.

Derek nods toward it. "Would you like me to see who it is?"

"No, no, I can do it. This is my home, after all."

I march up to the door, but before I can check the security camera, Derek clears his throat.

"Might want to pull your dress down, Ms. Sangster."

I feel my brows tightening, but when I glance down at my body, my jaw drops. "Oh, bollocks."

Yes, my dress is still hiked up over my hips.

Once I've yanked it down, I check the camera screen as the visitor rings the bell yet again. "Bugger me."

"Who is it?" Derek asks.

"Hugh and Avery."

The bloody man chuckles. "Great. Let them in."

I whirl around to give him my back and grasp the doorknob. Motion behind me and to my right spurs me to glance sideways at Derek.

He just plucked my knickers off the floor. Now, he stuffs them into his pocket and winks at me.

I swing the door open and paste on a professional smile. "Good morning. What are you two doing here on a Saturday morning?"

"Visiting you," Avery says. "Well, you and Derek. He told us his crew got food poisoning and he'd be with you all day. Hugh and I thought we'd keep you guys company."

Her smile seems a bit too cheery. Hugh seems a bit too casual. What are these two plotting? I'm older than the pair of them, which means I have the experience to realize when these youngsters are trying to interfere in my life.

Avery boosts up on her tiptoes and smiles even more cheerily. "There you are, Derek."

"Yeah, here I am."

Hugh clasps Avery's hand, then pushes past me while dragging his fiancee along with him. "Should we play games?"

I shut the door. "I don't own any games. Unless you enjoy the *Financial Times* crossword puzzle."

Hugh releases his fiancee's hand so he can dig something out of his trouser pocket. "Good thing I brought this."

The man is holding a deck of cards.

"I don't know any card games," I say, trying not to let my annoyance show in my voice. I still feel off balance after what Derek and I did moments ago. "If you're in a gaming mood, you'll need to go elsewhere."

"We'll teach you to play poker."

Derek looks at me, then speaks to Hugh. "I think Diana's not in the mood for a complicated card game. Maybe we should give up on that idea."

"Go fish is easy," Avery says.

He glances at me again, and something in my expression must have clued him in to the fact I'm uncomfortable with this entire situation. "We shouldn't be playing games, anyway. I'm here to do my job, not horse around. And I'm sure Diana has things she needs to do."

"I get why you're working on Saturday," Avery says. "But why would Diana need to slave away today? She deserves the weekend off. So do you. I'm sure we can all take one day to have a little fun. If not games, then how about lunch at a nice restaurant? You can guard Diana while we do that."

Derek looks at me yet again, but this time he raises his brows. "What do you think of that idea? You do need some downtime. You're the hardest working woman on the planet."

Avery and Hugh both stare at Derek. They seem surprised by what he said, though I can't imagine why. It was hardly a shocking statement. A bit of hyperbole, but not a shock. I'm sure there are other people on earth who work harder than I do.

Hugh clears his throat. "Are we going to lunch, then? It's a bit early for that, but we could take a walk along the river first for some fresh air."

Since it seems unlikely that our guests will leave without convincing us to do something with them today, I surrender. "Yes, a walk and lunch would be lovely."

Chapter Seven

Derek

Hugh and Avery have become so annoying lately, probably because they're drunk on pre-wedding bliss. I know how stubborn my sister can be, so I realized quickly that she wouldn't give up on the idea of spending the day with me and Diana. I really am working today. This isn't a play date, not for me. But once my baby sister roped her fiancé into whatever plan she devised, I knew there was no stopping the meddling train.

"I need to change clothes," Diana says. "This dress isn't appropriate for a walk."

"Sure it is," I say. "If you wear flats instead of heels."

Now I'm a fashion expert. Jeez, I just want to get this day over with so I can stop watching Hugh and Avery give us knowing looks and whisper to each other. Whatever they think they're meddling about, it's bullshit. If they screw up my plan to win Diana over, I'll strangle the pair of them.

Yeah, it's clear Diana is very uncomfortable.

"Let her wear whatever she wants," Avery says. "Since when do you care about her clothes? You're her bodyguard, not her fashion consultant."

"Well, uh, I—Never mind."

Diana hustles upstairs.

Hugh and Avery have dressed casually, and I imagine Diana will do the same. I didn't bring any extra clothes, which means I'll be the odd man out who's wearing a suit and tie.

Avery walks up to me and studies my suit. "You don't look like you're out for a walk along the river. At least take off your tie."

Yeah, my sister can sometimes read my mind. At least it feels that way. "I'm working, Avery. You three are the ones goofing off."

I kind of doubt Diana does "goofing off," but I couldn't think of anything else to say.

The woman herself comes down the stairs, and I can't help staring at her. Diana is wearing is the sweats she only ever puts on when she goes for her private walks along the Thames. She has her hands tucked into the pockets of her hoodie, and tennies cover her feet. But it's the scrunchy thing holding her hair back in a ponytail that has me reeling. The only time Diana ever pulls her hair back is during her twice-weekly walks. I've seen her this way many times before, but for some reason, it affects me differently today. For some reason? Sure, it's a big mystery. Not like I screwed her ten minutes ago.

With everyone else dressed for the weekend, I will stand out like a neon-pink flamingo. So I take off my tie and stuff it in my pants pocket. My fingers brush against lace. *Oh, shit.* That's Diana's panties in my pocket. With my tie in there too, my pocket now sports a conspicuous lump.

Diana glances at my hip. Her eyes widen, but only for half a second. She must've realized why that lump is there.

I toss my tie onto the sofa.

"Take off your jacket too," Avery suggests. "Then you'll seem more casual."

"I'm fine this way. Stop being bossy."

"Don't get grumpy with me."

"Can we just go?" I wave toward the door. "The river isn't in this building."

Hugh and Avery hold hands as they exit the flat, and Diana trails after them. But I maintain a slight distance behind her, the way a bodyguard should. Hugh drapes his arm around Avery's shoulders in the elevator and keeps nuzzling her neck while whispering things I can't hear and I'm pretty sure I don't want to hear even if I could.

Perfect. I get to spend the day watching those two nuzzle each other and exchange syrupy glances.

My gaze flicks to Diana. I'm standing right beside her, since the elevator isn't large. We had sex not that long ago. She screamed when she came. I loved the look on her face while we "shagged," as the Brits like to say, and I'd wanted to take her into the bedroom for another round. But she wouldn't have let me do that. For now, I'm allowing her to call the shots, but that won't last forever.

Diana glances at me, then swerves her attention to the wall.

Yeah, I've got a lot of work to do with her.

The second the elevator doors open, Hugh takes hold of Avery's hand again, and I go back to walking slightly behind Diana. We jog across the street and head down the sidewalk, which I think the Brits call the pavement, on our way to the river path. It's a beautiful day, sunny and warm, but not too warm. Just right for a romantic walk.

Only Hugh and Avery will experience that. Me, I'll be keeping an eye on Diana while trying not to stare at her ass. I also need to stop my brain from showing me replays of our encounter in the entryway of her flat.

What if she's pregnant already? Not sure what the odds are for hitting the jackpot the first time. She probably wouldn't know for a while yet even if we did succeed today.

Once we step onto the path, my sister decides to meddle again. She abandons her fiancé and sidles up to me, hooking her arm around mine. "We haven't had a good chat in quite a while."

"We talked this morning."

"But that wasn't a brother-sister chat."

I notice Hugh has slowed down to stroll along the path beside Diana. He starts talking to her, but I can't hear what they're saying. My sister has forced me to walk slower, so I'm further away from Diana than I would like—in terms of guarding her.

My sister nudges me in the side with her elbow. "Come on, you can tell me the truth."

"About what?"

"You and Diana."

"No idea what you're getting at." Okay, I do have my suspicions, but I'm hoping to hell she won't actually say it.

Avery bumps her shoulder into my upper arm. "You two are attracted to each other. Why don't you just ask her out?"

But of course, she did say it.

"I'm her bodyguard, that's all." I groan. "I knew you were trying to meddle. Did you catch that disease from Hugh? I hear all his buddies love to do that. Their wives must have brainwashed them."

"Being grumpy won't change anything. You have feelings for Diana. I can see it every time you look at her, and it's obvious every time she looks at you too."

"For pity's sake, Avery, butt out of my personal life."

"I don't remember you butting out when I first started dating Hugh."

Damn, I hate it when my sister is right. It's annoying. "That was different. Hugh called himself Lord Steamy and dragged you off to his family estate in the middle of nowhere."

"You came with us to Sommerleigh. And you liked him even then, so don't deny it."

"I tolerated him. We didn't really get to know each other until after the engagement party."

Avery gazes up at me with another one of those damn knowing smiles. "Hugh thinks you and Diana have already slept together."

"No, we haven't." Because she outlawed bedroom sex. My sister doesn't need to know that. "Why is Hugh contemplating my sex life, anyway? I hope your fiance isn't turning into a perv."

"Nice deflection, but I'm not buying it."

"Enough, Avery." I grasp her hand, drag her up to Hugh, and curl her arm around his. "Take your fiancee back, Lord Sticky. She misses you. I mean, it's been at least thirty seconds since you two nuzzled each other."

"I see Avery's plot has backfired," Hugh says. Then he pats Avery's arm. "I told you not to push so hard, darling. Stubborn people don't respond well to that sort of technique."

"I know all about stubborn men. You were way more pigheaded than Derek will be. I'm his sister, after all."

The happy couple slows down until they're walking well behind me and Diana, but I resume my position just behind her.

"You might as well walk beside me," she says with a sigh. "Those two won't stop until you do."

She's right, so I move up beside her. That ponytail bounces a little with every step she takes.

"I like the ponytail," I tell her. "It suits you."

She jerks as if I threw a dead bird at her. "Suits me? That's ridiculous."

"Why? You're always beautiful, but that scrunchy thing makes you look sweet."

She casts me a sideways glance, her lips curving up at one corner. "Please don't insult me that way. I have a tough-as-nails image to uphold."

"Your secret is safe with me, Ms. Sangster."

"We're taking the day off. That means you should call me Diana for now. In fact, I asked you to do that in my office."

"Right. You should call me Derek, then."

Hugh and Avery catch up to us and point out the restaurant they'd had in mind. It's a nice place, not fancy, just the kind of thing normal people enjoy. I might have learned a lot about Diana over the past few months, but I know very little about her food preferences. The menu includes everything from burgers to quiche and even oysters. I don't order those. When Hugh jokingly suggests he wants to order oysters for Avery, and he wags his eyebrows at me, I kick his shin under the table.

Well, he did ask for that. I don't need to hear about what he and my sister do to get turned on. I know Lord Sticky just likes to harass me, the way guys often do to each other.

I didn't kick him hard. It was really just a poke.

Hugh does not order oysters, which means I don't need to drag him into an alley and sucker punch him. He and Avery share a gigantic plate of pasta, but fortunately for my stomach, they don't feed each other. I would've barfed for sure if they did that. I love my sister, and I'm glad she's happy, but all the lovey-dovey stuff isn't for me.

I decide to eat a double-decker hamburger with all the fixings and a large side of French fries.

Diana orders the same thing, but with chili cheese fries and jalapeños.

I can't help gaping at her. "I can't believe you eat stuff like that. No woman I ever met likes hot peppers."

She shrugs. "I don't often eat this way, but I'm quite hungry. Ravenous, actually."

Ravenous? Yeah, I am too. But not for food.

When our meals arrive, I get to watch Diana Sangster consuming a hamburger with all the gusto of an inmate who just got released from prison. Oddly, that turns me on big time. A drop of ketchup slides down her chin, and I wish I could lick that off for her. But she daintily dabs it away with a napkin.

I want to drag her back to her flat or mine and eat all kinds of succulent treats off her body.

Stop thinking about sex, moron. Remember the plan.

Take it slow, give her time, don't push. That's my plan. But seeing another side of Diana makes it so damn hard for me to stick to my guns.

After lunch, Hugh and Avery climb into a taxi to go home. Diana and I grab a taxi too, though I can tell she doesn't like utilizing public transportation. She's used to her limo, but we didn't drive here, so she has to make do. I resist the urge to drape an arm around her shoulders or clasp her hand. Having sex with Diana, even if it only lasted thirty seconds, is screwing with my head.

Diana squirms in her seat and puckers her lips.

This isn't the most comfortable taxi I've ever been in. Is there such a thing as a comfortable taxi? Probably not.

"Pull over here," I tell the driver. "We can walk the rest of the way."

Diana swerves her attention to me, surprise widening her eyes.

"It's only two blocks away," I tell her. "What do you say?"

"Yes, let's walk."

Though she wants to pay the driver, I insist on taking care of that myself. It is kind of my fault that she got shanghaied by Hugh and Avery. My sister seems to have decided she needs to find me a girlfriend. I know Diana is a billionaire, but a gentleman should pay for meals or cab fares, at least once in a while.

We amble down the sidewalk, passing by another large, swanky apartment complex. This is a ritzy neighborhood with amazing views, but I prefer my much smaller flat several blocks away in a more normal part of town.

Diana's cell phone rings. She digs it out of her hoodie's pocket and checks who's calling. "I need to take this."

"Should I move away to give you privacy?"

"I don't think that will be necessary."

Just as she lowers her finger to the screen to take the call, a figure dashes out from behind a parked car and pushes between me and Diana. She stumbles into the parked car. I stagger backwards.

"He took my mobile," Diana shouts.

Without even thinking about it, I bolt down the street after the thief.

Chapter Eight

Diana

I stand frozen, helpless to do anything but watch as Derek races after the thief, who slams into a burly man. That slows the thief down enough that Derek can catch up to the wanker and grab the back of his shirt, yanking him to a halt. Derek spins the man around so he can snatch my mobile out of the thief's hand while gripping the man's arm with his other hand.

"What the fuck do you think you're doing?" Derek snarls. "You slimy little—"

The thief kicks Derek in the groin. While Derek doubles over briefly, the wanker sprints around a corner, out of sight. But my bodyguard does not give up. He straightens, hardens his expression, and bolts after the thief.

For reasons I can't explain, I run after him.

I've just rounded the corner when I see Derek and the thief. My bodyguard has snagged the wanker's wrists and now holds them behind his back, held in place by Derek's hand. No cuffs required.

He yanks the thief's wrists, making his arms jerk too. "I'm calling the cops, you worthless piece of shit. Assaulting a woman? Stealing from her? I should pound on you until you're nothing but a lump of ground meat."

The nasty snarl in Derek's voice sends a shiver up my spine, but it's not a fear response. That shiver feels warm and tingly in the most sensual manner. I can handle myself, but I like knowing Derek Hahn is always there to tackle a toerag for me.

He tosses me my mobile. "Call the cops."

I start to dial, but I don't need to bother. A bobby has just jogged out of a coffee shop. He halts between me and Derek, his brows hiking up when he notices the thief.

"What's going on here?" the bobby asks.

Before I can speak, Derek steps in. "This little shit"—He nods toward the man he holds captive—"stole that woman's cell phone. He assaulted her and me."

"You shouldn't have pursued the chap on your own."

"That woman is Diana Sangster, the business mogul. And I'm her bodyguard, Derek Hahn." My hero pulls his ID out of his hip pocket and hands it to the bobby. "Check my credentials. I'm the CEO of Protection Services International and a licensed close protection officer in the UK, as well as in the US."

The bobby seems impressed, and though he glances at Derek's identification, he quickly hands it back to him. "I know who Ms. Sangster is. I'll take this man into custody." He looks at me. "Sorry I didn't recognize you at first, Ms. Sangster. I think everyone knows you now, after you saved Sommerleigh Sweets. My wife loves your candies."

"I didn't save it alone," I say. "Hugh Parrish is the CEO and the driving force behind his family's company."

The bobby takes custody of the thief and asks us to go with him to the police station so he can take our statements. A few bystanders who saw the altercation volunteer to do the same. Derek and I climb into a taxi for the ride to the police station.

I'm still holding my phone in my hand. As I gaze down at it, I suddenly remember who had been ringing me when the thief appeared. It was Pippa.

"I need to make a call," I tell Derek. "I never did speak to the person who rang me. It is personal, as I said before."

"No problem." He pulls a pair of earbuds out of his pocket and hooks them up to his mobile. "I can listen to music while you take care of your personal call."

"Thank you." He honestly is the most considerate man I've ever met.

I dial Pippa's number.

She answers on the first ring. "Diana? You must be working on the weekend again. That's the only reason you wouldn't answer when I rang you."

"No, I'm not working." But I don't want to tell her about the thief. She would worry about me. "I'm sorry I didn't answer. Is something wrong?"

"Why are you whispering?"

Despite knowing Derek is listening to music and most likely can't hear me, I realize I have been whispering. "I'm in a taxi. Now please tell me, is there something wrong?"

"Sort of." She hesitates, and I know she must be biting the inside of her lip. Pippa always does that when she's nervous. "I don't like it here. I have some friends, but they aren't good mates, and nobody really wants to talk to me. May I please come home, Diana?"

I miss her too, and I would love for Pippa to come home. But there's the problem of Derek and our arrangement. I'll need time to devise a plan for bringing Pippa home without causing a commotion—or worse, having Pippa realize that Derek and I are more than colleagues. I sent her to boarding school because I thought it might be good for her, and so she wouldn't worry about why I have bodyguards now. I did not do that so she wouldn't meet Derek and realize that he and I have…chemistry.

She might be fourteen, but Pippa is a very clever girl.

Do I actually need bodyguards? It's doubtful. I can't explain why I hired Derek's company. It had seemed like the right thing at the time.

"Let me sort some plans," I tell her. "But yes, pet, you can come home soon. I promise."

"Brilliant! Thank you, Diana."

"Goodbye, dear."

I ring off and glance at Derek.

His gaze flicks to me, and he smiles.

I pluck one of his earbuds out of his ear. "My call is done."

Derek tucks his earbuds back into his pocket. "Everything okay? You looked kind of tense while you were talking. I couldn't hear what you said, but I couldn't help noticing your demeanor."

"There is nothing to worry about."

"Glad to hear it."

He isn't going to question me about my mysterious call. Well, discretion is a large part of his job. Maybe I am slightly disappointed that he didn't try to wheedle the information out of me. But no, that would be ridiculous. I don't give a toss if Derek does or does not interrogate me about my call.

And I absolutely do not wish he would figure out my secret.

Once we've provided our statements to the police, we head home in another taxi. I slip off my shoes and drop onto the sofa. Derek goes into the kitchen and returns ten minutes later with two steaming cups of tea.

I accept the cup he offers me. "I thought you didn't like tea. You are a coffee man."

"Yeah, but Hugh got me hooked on Earl Grey. I have a cup now and then."

"Are you becoming British?"

He chuckles as he sits down at the opposite end of the sofa. "No danger of that. I do like bangers and mash, though mostly because I love to turn that phrase into innuendo."

"Innuendo? Based on sausage and mashed potatoes?"

"Oh, yeah. Wanna see how?" He sets his teacup on the end table and slides closer to me. Then he speaks in a deeper, softer tone. "I'd love to massage those potatoes until they're creamy and silky, then steam the sausage until it glistens with its own juices."

Why am I suddenly breathing harder? He's talking about food, not shagging.

He shimmies even closer and lays his arm across the sofa's back. "When I roll that sausage over, I'll rub spices into its skin, using my fingertips to gently caress the casing."

"No one handles sausage that way." Now I sound slightly breathless, and I feel warm all over while slickness gathers between my thighs.

Derek lowers his head until his lips graze my ear. "I'll get some butter and hold it in my hand until it starts to soften and warm up, dribbling between my fingers. Then I'll lay it in the pan and lick my fingers clean while I watch that butter melt for me."

His demonstration of innuendo has transformed into seduction. I should tell him to leave off, but I can't convince my vocal cords to work. My body wants him to do to me all the things he's saying about food. I would melt for him so easily, and that fact unnerves me. But the desire rising inside me overpowers my unease.

"I'll use only sweet cream butter," he murmurs. "The sausage and potatoes will be drenched with it. I could eat those bangers and mash straight out of the pan, using my fingers to devour every last bit."

Can't speak. Can't move. Perhaps I desperately want him to do everything he just described, and do it on my body, but I can't let him. That would violate our deal. We are having sex only so I can get pregnant. That means we do not need to indulge in the kind of steamy, sensual love-making that he has just visualized for me.

"Bangers are my favorite," he whispers. "Don't you love them too? They're so thick and long, and they slide—"

"That's enough, Derek." My breathless tone seems unlikely to convince him I mean that.

"Mm," he murmurs. "If you made this meal for me, it would taste so damn good. Maybe one day you'll take my bangers into your mouth and eat them up."

I know what he means. And I experience a disturbingly powerful urge to give him what he suggested by swallowing his cock, right here on the sofa.

He skims his lips down my cheek, stopping millimeters from my mouth. "No reason why we can't have fun while getting you knocked up."

"I told you—"

The doorbell rings.

My heart thuds, and I spring to my feet.

Derek sighs and slumps against the sofa. "What's going on today? You never get this many guests."

"How would you know? You don't normally protect me on the weekends."

"But my people report back to me about that stuff. It's all part of ensuring you get the best security possible."

"Oh. Yes, that makes sense."

I whirl around, intending to jog toward the door, but I trip over the end table and nearly fall down.

The front door swings open, then slams shut.

Derek has just caught me around the waist to halt my fall.

Pippa pushes the door shut and turns toward the living room. Her jaw goes slack, and her eyes widen a touch as she takes in the sight of me and Derek. But her lips tick up in a mischievous little smile.

I stumble sideways to shake off Derek's arm. Straightening my spine and my clothes, I hurry over to Pippa. "What are you doing here? I said I would make arrangements."

She hunches her shoulders. "I didn't want to wait, so I used the last of my allowance to buy a bus ticket. Please don't send me back."

"We will discuss this later."

Her gaze moves past me, and she smiles in that mischievous way again. "Who is that?"

My bodyguard marches over to us and offers Pippa his hand. "Derek Hahn. Diana didn't mention she had a daughter as pretty as she is."

Pippa blushes a little as she shakes his hand. "I'm Pippa. Diana is my aunt."

"Really?" Derek glances at me. "How come you never told me about your niece?"

I huff. "Because it's none of your concern. Pippa, please go upstairs. I need to talk to Derek."

"My suitcases are in the hall. The bellman brought them up for me."

"I'll take care of that," Derek says. "Just be a minute."

He rushes to open the door, then picks up all four of Pippa's large suitcases and carries them inside. As he kicks the door shut, he asks, "Where should I put these?"

I wave toward the stairs. "In the other bedroom."

He marches up the stairs while still holding all four suitcases.

Pippa's eyes go wide again. "Wow. He can carry all of that stuff."

A sensuous tingle sweeps over my skin, but I manage not to sound like a breathless schoolgirl when I speak. "Yes, he's very strong. But you and I need to have a serious conversation, Pippa."

Her shoulders sag. "Yeah, I figured I'm in trouble."

I clasp her shoulder and urge her to walk into the living room. We both sit down on the sofa. "Why did you run away from the school?"

"Because I don't like being so far from you. I know it's only four hours away, but I'd rather be here."

What can I say to that? She sounds forlorn. I never discussed with her whether she wanted to go away, but instead declared that she would. Why did I do that? I had convinced myself that it would be best for her if she went away and didn't need to know that I now have bodyguards. Pippa would wonder why, and it might frighten her. To spare her the anxiety, I banished her.

I suddenly realize I need to notify the school that Pippa is here with me. Doing that only takes a few minutes and a good amount of apologizing. When the head mistress asks when Pippa will return to school, I think of only one reasonable response. "We haven't decided yet, but Pippa will spend the week with me."

That statement makes Pippa smile so brightly that I get a pang in my chest.

Derek jogs back down the stairs.

Tonight, in my flat with Derek and Pippa, I suddenly realize all my excuses are bollocks. But I don't dare consider the real reasons for what I did to Pippa.

"I'm starved," the girl says, while holding a hand over her belly. "Could we have bangers and mash for dinner?"

Derek smirks.

And I wince.

Chapter Nine

Derek

I shouldn't think it's funny that Diana seems embarrassed because Pippa just suggested eating bangers and mash. But the billionaire businesswoman rarely lets anyone see how she feels, and I like that one kid could do that to her. Of course, she might actually be reeling because we'd been thirty seconds away from fucking on the sofa when her niece walked into the flat.

Diana has family? She never mentioned that. Why would she? I'm just her bodyguard and baby donor.

For now.

Diana jumps up and hurries over to the kitchen island, though she seems to have no idea why she did that. So she turns around and leans against the island.

Pippa hurries over there and sidles up to Diana while clasping her hands, raising them in a pleading gesture. "Please, Diana, please. We never had bangers and mash at school. The food was bloody awful there."

"Don't use foul language. You are a child."

The girl rolls her eyes. "I'm fourteen. Besides, the B-word isn't really foul language. You say it all the time."

A laugh barks out of me before I get the chance to squelch it. "Diana curses all the time? Not when I'm around. She always behaves like a perfect lady."

Pippa swings her attention to me, then to Diana, then back to me. "Does she really act that way? She must like you a lot. Are you her boyfriend?"

Diana makes a sound that's almost a growl. "No, he is not. Go to your room, Pippa, and change out of that ruddy uniform."

"You just swore again," the girl says with a grin.

"The word ruddy is not swearing." Diana swats her niece's bottom. "Go. Now."

Pippa skips over to the stairs while grinning, pauses to glance back at us, then hurries up to the top floor.

I walk over to Diana and lean my hip against the island beside her. "Why didn't ever mention that you have a niece?"

"Because that's part of my private life. I keep her away from business dealings."

"How long has Pippa been away at boarding school?"

She eyes me sideways. "What does that matter?"

"I'd like to know, that's all. You can tell me to shut my mouth and I will. But I'd like us to be friends, considering what I've agreed to do for you. And friends share stuff."

Diana shuts her eyes and exhales a long sigh. "I sent Pippa away three months ago."

"Right before you hired my company to protect you?"

She nods.

"You told me at the time that you didn't have any threats against yourself, that you only wanted bodyguards just in case."

"That's true."

I move closer to her. "But you sent your niece to boarding school."

"Not because I feared for her safety."

"Why, then?"

She bites the inside of her lip, just like I saw Pippa do, and wraps her arms around herself. "I didn't want—I believed boarding school would be good for her."

That's bullshit, I'm sure. But she doesn't want to tell me, not yet, and I won't push too hard today. I want to know where Pippa's parents are, but I won't push about that either. Those questions can wait. Diana is clearly frazzled by her niece's sudden appearance. Her confusion is cute.

Yeah, feeling that way probably makes me an ass. But I swear she's never seemed more likable than she does now. The tough-as-nails shell has cracked.

Pippa comes skipping down the stairs.

I've never seen anyone do that. How the kid can skip down those steps without falling is beyond me.

She halts in front of us. "We could all make bangers and mash together. Doesn't that sound like fun?"

"Yes, pet," Diana says, though she doesn't sound enthusiastic about the idea. Her slumped posture matches her tone of voice. "Let's do that."

I lean toward Diana and whisper, "She meant the three of us, you know."

"Yes, I know," she hisses out of the corner of her mouth.

Pippa skips around the island and stops at the fridge. "Come on, you guys, hurry up. I'm ready to pass out from starvation."

I study Diana's sweats, then examine what Pippa is wearing. And I can't help chuckling. "You two have matching outfits."

Diana thrusts herself away from the island and scowls at me. "It was Pippa's idea."

She stalks around the island to the fridge and helps Pippa gather what we need.

I amble over there and start hunting around for a frying pan inside the cabinets.

"What are you doing?" Diana says. "You're making a bloody racket down there."

"I'm trying to find a frying pan."

"Look up," Pippa says.

When I glance back at her, she's pointing toward the ceiling. That's when I see it. Pots and pans hang from hooks up there. "Oh, yeah. Now I get it. Thanks, kiddo."

As we collect everything we'll need, I tell dumb jokes to make Pippa laugh. At first, Diana ignores the fun we're having, but eventually, she stops pretending that she doesn't want to joke around with us and starts teasing me and Pippa. God, she's beautiful when she's like this. Relaxed, open, free, full of life. I get why she feels like she needs to be tough at work, but she even acts that way around me and Hugh and Avery outside of the office.

I'm glad I get to see something in her that few people do.

When I toss a "banger" into the frying pan and then slap a big old pat of butter in there too, Diana smirks at me. I'm sure she's flashing back to what I whispered in her ear on the sofa earlier.

And I can't resist smirking right back at her.

"You two have to be dating," Pippa says. "My friend Melora says when people look at each other while smiling, it means they have a crush. And that word means they like each other."

"I know what a crush is," Diana says. "Derek is a good man, a colleague and a friend."

Now Pippa is smirking. "I meant you *like* like each other."

I flip the sausage over and smear more butter in the pan. "Should we start singing the K-I-S-S-I-N-G song?"

"Ooh, yes!" Pippa almost shrieks. "I knew you were Diana's boyfriend."

I raise my hands while still holding the spatula. "No, hey, I didn't mean that. I was just teasing Diana."

The woman in question has gone stoic, which means she's pissed at me, I think. Either that, or she's terrified. Not sure which is worse.

"The sausage is ready," I say. "If you girls have the potatoes finished, then we can eat."

Pippa holds up a bowl of mashed potatoes. "Aren't these beautiful? I've never seen Diana whip anything as fast as she did these."

Yeah, she was probably a whipping maniac because she's freaked out about this whole situation. The woman who guards her privacy like it's the Hope Diamond just got smacked in the face with her private life. Honestly, I don't understand why she felt the need to hide Pippa from anybody. She's a sweet kid.

After dinner, we hang out in the living room. I offered to leave, but Pippa fake pouted and said "please, please, please" in a fake whiny voice until Diana agreed that I should stay. Pippa wanted to play the British version of Monopoly, and that sounded like fun to me. Diana bowed out of the game to watch the news on TV. Business news, naturally. An hour of hearing about boring stock market stuff and mind-numbing chatter about currency trading or something makes my brain hurt even when I'm only subconsciously absorbing it.

While Diana stares at the TV, Pippa and I have a great time. When the kiddo buys her fourth hotel, she throws her arms up and shouts "woo-hoo." And I swear Diana smiles the tiniest bit, though she keeps her gaze aimed at the TV.

"Come and join us, Diana," I say. "The more the merrier."

"I don't indulge in merriment."

Pippa's brows furrow. "Of course you do. At Christmas, you always dress up as Lady Santa Claus and do your comedy routine."

I gape at Diana. "You do comedy?"

"Oh yeah," Pippa says. "Diana is so funny. You should see her in a white beard and with a pillow under the Santa suit to give her a big belly. Then she says 'ho-ho-ho' and grabs the plate of cookies I made for her and she—"

"Enough, Pippa," Diana says. "Derek does not want to hear about that."

I grin. "Oh yes I do. Bring out the Santa suit, Ms. Sangster."

Pippa slumps against the sofa. "She won't do it. Diana is uptight most of the time. Maybe you could tell a joke to make her laugh."

"Let's cut her some slack."

"All right. But it's a great story."

"I'm sure it is."

Diana in a Santa suit? I can't picture that, though I'd love to see it sometime.

"Time for bed, Pippa," Diana says. "Go upstairs and get ready. I'll be up shortly to make sure you actually go to bed. No watching films on your mobile."

Pippa rolls her eyes but obeys Diana's command, hurrying upstairs. She disappears from view, then hollers, "You two can snog now if you want. I'll be in my room."

Diana's brows cinch up. "How does that child know what snogging is? She's too young for that."

I sit down beside her on the sofa. "Uh, what is snogging?"

"Kissing. Making out, more precisely."

"Brits have the cutest words for things. But I wouldn't worry about how Pippa knows what snogging is. She probably just picked that up from one of her friends."

"She's fourteen. Soon, she'll have boyfriends." Diana tucks her legs under her. "Not sure I can handle that."

"I'm sure. A strong, capable woman like you can deal with anything."

She bows her head. "In business, yes. The rest of life is what trips me up. But I could not stand it if I ruined Pippa's life."

Her shoulders have caved in, and she picks at her sweatpants. She had removed her scrunchy thing earlier, and her hair has now fallen over her face. I've never seen Diana like this—vulnerable and scared. Everyone has issues that make them anxious, but I guess I've assumed since the day we met that nothing could knock her off balance. In the past few days, I've learned that's not true. She's human after all, and that makes me want her even more, and not just for sex.

She sucks in a ragged breath and exhales it.

I crook a finger under her chin and lift gently until I can see her face again. She won't look at me. That's okay. I can tell her what I need to say without eye-to-eye contact. "Diana, you could never ruin Pippa's life. She's a smart, strong, amazing girl, and I'd bet she learned all of that from you."

"But I don't want her to be like me. She's full of light and joy. If my rigidness rubs off on her…"

I had no idea she worried so much. Diana does a fantastic job of hiding it. She has her hand on her knee, so I lay mine on top of it. "We're friends, remember? You can talk to me about anything and I'll listen. I won't give advice unless you want it, but you are not alone, Diana. Avery and Hugh are your friends too, if you'll let them get to know you the way I have."

"You don't know me."

"Not as well as a friend should, but we can fix that. I'd bet I already know you better than anyone else on earth. I've watched over you for three months and learned all your habits."

Her lips curve up the littlest bit. "I suppose you do."

"See? We're friends." With the weirdest kind of benefits. But hey, I agreed to her baby deal, so I can't complain. "Pippa coming home knocked you off kilter, but you'll adjust."

She tilts her head to the side, studying me as if she's never seen me before. "You aren't the way I assumed you were."

"Is that good or bad?"

Diana just smiles with her lips sealed.

No idea what that means. But I think we've developed some kind of bond. I don't know what that means either.

"You should go home," she says. "I'll see you on Monday. I'm sure Wesley and Sheldon will be able to resume their duties tomorrow, and I'll be fine overnight. You've earned some time off."

I don't want a day off, not anymore. But she's the boss, when it comes to deciding what kind of protection she wants, and I need to respect that. I get up, then impulsively bend over to kiss her forehead. "Good night, Diana."

Then I walk out the door.

Chapter Ten

Diana

Saturday had rushed by in a blur, but Sunday seemed to drag on forever. Wesley and Sheldon did indeed return to their posts yesterday, and they executed their duties with professionalism and decorum, as usual. Might I have hoped that Derek would give them the day off and stay with me in their stead? Possibly. A little bit. I don't understand what happened on Saturday, between me and Derek, but I know it irrevocably altered our dynamic.

I told him things I shouldn't have. Personal things.

That will never happen again.

Monday morning has finally arrived, and I've conscripted Avery to serve as my babysitter for the morning. I told Pippa she could have the week off and that we would discuss her school situation during this time, but I need to handle some business matters first. Avery was more than happy to serve as Pippa's minder. I won't ask her to do that again, though. She has her own business to attend to, as well as a wedding coming up on Saturday. She and Hugh have invited Pippa to the big event. I'd already been on the guest list.

I've just sat down at my desk when the door swings open—and Derek saunters up to me. He spins my chair toward him. "Get up, Diana. We have work to do."

"Yes, I'm aware of that. Why do you think I'm sitting at my desk? To work, obviously."

He shakes his head. "Not that kind of work."

"What are you on about?"

"Our deal." He rests his hands atop my chair and leans in so close that I can smell his aftershave and feel his breaths teasing my lips. His voice drops to a whisper. "I'm talking about the baby-making work we need to do. One time might not get it done. We need to screw over and over."

"Well, yes, but—"

"No wriggling out of it. You want a baby, I'm providing the donations. That means"—He leans in even more, his lips grazing mine—"we need to fuck again, right now."

"Once a week is enough."

"Uh-uh-uh. If you want to get a bun in the oven, we need to do lots of baking."

"Why are you using a moronic baking metaphor? I am not an oven."

He drags one finger down my face, from my temple to the corner of my mouth, and suddenly, I have trouble catching my breath. "I'll make you so hot for me that you'll feel like you've been thrust into an oven. But first, I'll knead you like dough until you rise for me."

"You clearly know nothing about baking bread."

"But you like what I'm saying even when it's moronic." He drags that finger over my chin and down my throat. "Your pupils are dilated. That means you're turned on. So let's get started with the next round of baby-making."

"Not in my office."

He studies me for a moment, then straightens and holds out his hand, palm up. "Okay, let's do it somewhere else."

"I can't leave the building. I have a meeting in thirty minutes."

Derek smiles with devious intent. "You think I can't get us both off in less than thirty minutes? Trust me, I've learned every way to make a woman come faster than she ever thought was possible. Remember Saturday in the entryway?"

Oh yes, I remember that. Even if I live to be a hundred, I will never forget what we did in the entryway. "You seem awfully certain of your skills."

"Yep. I'm the best bodyguard you'll ever have, and I'm the only man for the baby-making job." He wiggles his fingers, urging me to take his hand. "Get up, Diana. I know exactly where we can go in this building."

This baby pact was my idea, so I can't very well back out of it now. And yes, I did enjoy our interlude in the entryway. But that was just sex. He is not getting under my skin. Everyone knows my flesh is made of cast iron.

I accept his hand and his help in rising from my chair. "All right. You are in charge of this mission."

"A mission to make you come and hopefully make a baby too."

"I've told you before that pleasure is irrelevant."

"Uh-huh." He keeps hold of my hand as he leads me toward the door. "But you don't mind if I give you that pleasure, do you? Don't remember you saying 'please stop, Derek, I don't want an orgasm.' Though you did beg me to—"

"Enough." I wrench my hand free of his, which takes more effort than I would've liked. He didn't refuse to release my hand. No, I simply couldn't let go until I forced myself to do it.

Derek guides me down the long hallway, past Hugh's office and various other rooms, and straight to the end. He halts in front of a nondescript door.

I shake my head when I see the sign on the door. "The janitorial closet?"

"You said not in your office. This is the only other place in this building that I know of where nobody else will go. The janitorial staff starts work really early and does this floor first, so they're gone by this time." He pushes the door open. "Step on in."

"What if the janitorial staff return to get more supplies?"

"They won't. Every floor has its own closet full of janitorial goodies." He opens the door wider and walks inside, flicking a switch to turn on a bare light bulb that hangs from the ceiling. "No more excuses. Get in here so I can make my next donation."

How does he turn the word donation into the most erotic thing I've ever heard? I wish he wouldn't say that word anymore. But I doubt that would help. Everything he says makes me want to tear his clothes off and do things to him that I've never done before.

Sex in a janitorial closet counts as one of those things.

I shuffle into the tiny room.

Derek shuts the door and backs me up to the wall beside it. He rests one arm on the wall as he unzips his trousers. "I've got a new innuendo for you."

"If it's food-related, I'd rather not hear it."

"But you got so turned on when I whispered my bangers and mash innuendo to you."

"Maybe I did, but once was enough for that metaphor. I am not mashed potatoes."

"No, you're not." He frees his cock, then pushes his hand under my skirt. "Thank you for not wearing slacks today. Makes it much easier for me to take you in a closet. And I love reaching under your skirt to do this."

He grasps my knickers and yanks them so hard that the lacy fabric rips.

I gasp. "Those knickers cost three hundred pounds. Do you enjoy destroying expensive designer clothing? I should lock my closet at home or you might shred my nightgown too."

"So, you're planning to invite me into your bedroom and your closet. I'd love to make you scream in there."

"No, I didn't mean—Ugh. I simply meant that—" I let my head fall back against the wall. "Never mind. Just get on with the proceedings, please."

"Proceedings?" he says with a laugh. "Never heard anybody describe sex that way before."

Derek crumples my destroyed knickers in his hand, then stuffs them into his trouser pocket. "I bet you're already hot for me and ready to go. Did you get slick and slippery as soon as I walked into your office? Or had you been fantasizing about me while you sat at your desk waiting for me?"

"I was not waiting for you. How could I know when you might turn up?"

He grins. "You *were* waiting for me, hey? I like that. And just so you know, I dreamed about you all night. Those were the hottest wet dreams I ever had."

I grasp his stiff cock and start pumping. "Are you planning to fuck me sometime today?"

He releases a deep, guttural groan as his eyes drift partway closed. "That's the first time you've ever touched my dick. Feels good, but you'd better stop. I'm supposed to come inside you, remember?"

"Of course I remember." Hiking up my skirt, I spread my legs. "Do it now."

"Yes, ma'am, Ms. Sangster."

He sets both arms on the wall and plunges his length into my body. My word, I've never felt anything as good as when Derek Hahn consumes me with his cock. I can't help moaning with pleasure as he fills me up, diving as deep inside me as he possibly can. I grasp his shoulders and hang on, just waiting for the climax I know will rock me to the core of my being. It's ludicrous. But I don't care.

"What's going on in there?" a male voice calls out. "Do you need medical attention?"

Derek growls under his breath.

The man outside tries to open the door.

But Derek slams his palm onto the door to keep it shut, while still fucking me. "Cleaning up vomit in here, pal. Get lost."

"Sorry. Sure you don't need medical attention?"

"Positive," Derek snarls.

Footsteps recede.

What if someone else hears us and we get caught? I should care about that. But I don't have the brainpower to understand the consequences, because Derek is pumping harder now. The idea that we might get caught intensified my arousal. Now I grow even more aroused as Derek nails me to the wall with every thrust and increases the pace, while the wet sucking sound created by our bodies grows louder. That sound alone could almost make me come, but the intense look on Derek's face combined with the power of his thrusts pushes me over the edge.

My mouth opens, and a scream will burst out of me any second, but I can't stop that from happening. Everyone on this floor will likely hear me.

Derek crushes his mouth to mine, swallowing my cry.

My body grips his cock in wave after wave as the orgasm grips me so hard that it finally chokes off my cries. But Derek keeps his mouth fastened to mine, pushing his tongue deep while he pounds into me like a jackhammer and finally comes.

Neither of us moves a muscle, not even once we've both finished. Our mouths remain glued to each other, and our breaths bluster out of our nostrils. His gaze bores straight into mine. I let his deep blue irises transfix me, but honestly, I would've been mesmerized even if he'd pulled away. What this man does to me...I can't describe it. Can't explain it.

And I will never tell him about it.

Because I know what he really wants from me. Derek Hahn wants a relationship, a real one, more than just sex for the purpose of having a baby. I can't go down the relationship road ever again. If Derek wound up hating me...

No. Never again.

Pippa is all I need. Well, Pippa and the baby I want to add to our little family.

Derek finally peels his mouth away from mine and staggers backward. The loss of his body heat—of his body, full stop—leaves me dazed for a moment. I must be pregnant by now, mustn't I? Perhaps I should have calculated my most fertile days this month, but I hadn't thought that far ahead. Once Derek agreed to my plan, all I could think about was when and where we would shag.

No, not when we would shag. When and where he would provide the donation.

He wipes a hand over his mouth. "Damn, that was even hotter than the first time."

Yes, it was. But I can't tell him that. My brain won't let me, even if I'd wanted to say the words. So instead, I tug my skirt down and try to comb my hair out with my fingers. I still tingle deep inside, and I can feel warm liquid trickling down my inner thighs. But I ignore all of that and clear my throat. "Thank you for the donation. Good day."

I march to the door and pull it open.

A large hand slams it shut. Derek's body brushes against my backside. "You're in denial, aren't you? This time was even better than the first, and that freaks you out. I get it. But don't act like I'm your human turkey baster."

"Must you always be so crude? You are the donor, that's all."

He presses his lips to my throat. "You can hold on to your denial as long as you want." He backs away. "Go on. Get back to work, Ms. Sangster."

I open the door and take one step.

A large hand thrusts my ruined knickers in my face. "Don't forget these, Ms. Sangster."

I snatch them away and hurry down the hall.

Chapter Eleven

Derek

I spend the rest of the day fighting against what my body wants me to do—find Diana and fuck her again. Every time I think about her, my dick starts to firm up. So, I bury myself in work instead of inside Diana's body and finish my entire schedule for all my employees for the next six months. I do that before eleven o'clock. Then I devise a plan to test the security in this building, since I'm the head of security in addition to running my own protection company, and that gets me through until noon.

Now what?

I get a lucky break that solves my problem. I don't need to search for another task to do because my sister conveniently calls me with a command.

"You're taking the rest of the week off," she says. "No griping, no wriggling out of it, no excuses. I'm getting married on Saturday, in case you've forgotten, and Hugh and I have decided to make it a week-long party at Sommerleigh."

"Sorry, I can't do that. Even if I'm excused from my duties as the head of security at Sommerleigh Sweets, I still have my private security firm. And my top client contracted for round-the-clock protection."

"You mean Diana. She already agreed to take the week off, so you have no more excuses. You can do your job even better at Sommerleigh since there are no muggers on the estate." Avery's voice takes on a sneaky tone. "We've already assigned your quarters in Sommerleigh House. You and Diana will be in adjoining rooms."

"Why? She wants her privacy, you know."

"But you are her bodyguard." My sister still sounds way too sneaky, and I'm getting a niggling in my gut that warns me she's up to something. "You'll want to stay as close to her as possible. Right?"

"Uh-huh. Do not meddle in any way, shape, or form."

"Meddling? Me?" She clucks her tongue. "You should know better by now."

"Does that mean you won't meddle?"

She hums tunelessly in the way I know means she's avoiding answering my question. "By the way, Pippa helped us pack some bags for Diana, and Hugh and I grabbed everything you might need along with some new clothes too."

"Fantastic. Hugh probably picked out baggy cargo pants and pastel T-shirts for me. The kind that have unicorns and kittens on them." I think about how Diana might react to this cockamamie idea, then realize my sister never answered my question. "Tell me now, Avery. You are not going to meddle, right?"

She says nothing for about two seconds. "Oh, look at the time. Gotta go. We'll pick you guys up at noon."

Avery hangs up on me.

I never got the chance to ask where I'm supposed to meet her or why she said that she and Lord Sticky would pick "us" up. I hope that doesn't mean Diana. She probably needs more than a few hours away from me. Our second round of quick and dirty sex seemed to make her even more anxious about our deal.

Maybe giving her time to adjust is the wrong play. Maybe I need to show her that I can be more than the guy who donates the, uh, stuff she needs. Okay, yeah, I still don't like thinking the S-word, much less speaking it. Does any guy like to talk about his little swimmers? I doubt it.

Women love to talk about "that time of the month."

I let my team know I'll be taking the week off and fiddle around with my computer for a while after that, then it's time to head downstairs and meet my sister and her hubby-to-be. I assume I should go downstairs, at any rate. If they get all lovey-dovey again in the car, I might slam my head into the door frame to knock myself out. Maybe I'm a little jealous that Avery and Hugh are so happy, and maybe that's because the woman I want insists my only role in her life is to get her pregnant. This is Avery's big week, though, and I will behave like a responsible adult.

As I walk out of the building, I see the limo with Hugh and Avery standing beside it. And I see Diana standing there too.

When she notices me, she winces.

Oh, perfect. Avery and Hugh must not have warned her I was coming along on this forced vacation in the English countryside.

My suspicions are confirmed when Avery throws her arms up and shouts, "Surprise!"

I glare at her, but she just keeps grinning.

Hugh wears a slightly pinched expression, like maybe he wasn't totally on board for this kidnapping scheme. He opens the rear door of the limo and spreads an arm. "Ladies first."

Diana and Avery climb into the car.

I approach Hugh and whisper, "This was Avery's idea, wasn't it?"

"Yes. Be prepared for more meddling once we reach Sommerleigh. Guests will be arriving all week, but you and Diana are the first."

"Can't you talk Avery out of poking her nose into my life?"

Hugh gives me a wry smile. "You were there when she pushed her pretty little nose into my life and turned it upside down. What makes you think I have any sway over her when it comes to helping you? She wants her brother to be happy—whether you like it or not."

I groan. Then I get into the limo.

Avery sits on the bench seat that faces the front, while Diana has taken the bench across from her that faces the rear. Diana sits on the edge of the seat with her fingers curled over its edge, seeming like she might bolt any second.

When I try to settle onto the seat beside my sister, she smacks my arm. "I'm sitting with Hugh. And it's my wedding week, so you can't complain about that."

"Right. The bride is the dictator. Should I bow down at your feet?"

"That won't be necessary. Just sit with Diana."

I move onto the opposite bench but leave a good gap between me and Diana.

Hugh climbs in, snuggling up to Avery, and the limo starts rolling.

Diana scoots as far away from me as she can get and stares out the tinted windows.

I glance around. "Hey, where's Pippa?"

"She wanted to take Sommerleigh Sweets factory tour," Hugh says. "She was rather excited about it. After that, my cousin Rupert will bring Pippa to Sommerleigh House along with his wife and their children. Their daughter is only a year older than Pippa, so they should get on well."

"For sure. Pippa's a sweet kid." I relax against the bench and drape my arm across it, careful not to touch Diana, and hook one ankle over the other knee. "So, how long will this trip to Lord Sticky's home take? At least you ponied up for a limo this time instead of making me play sardine in the backseat of your Jag."

Hugh lifts one brow. "I have never forced you to ride in the backseat."

"No, but I figured you'd want Avery up front with you nowadays, considering that she's your fiancee. Besides, you love trying to yank my chain, not that it ever works." I glance sideways at Diana, but she's still staring out the window. "Are you ever going to tell me how long this trip will take?"

"You've been to Sommerleigh many times. You ought to know the answer."

"Can't remember, can you?" I shake my head. "Sure you want to marry this guy, Avery? I think Hugh is developing Alzheimer's."

My sister flings both arms around her fiance and gives him what seems like an extra firm squeeze. It makes him wince just a little. "Hugh has an excellent memory."

"The trip will take a bit longer than usual," Hugh says, "because this limousine can't go as fast as my Jaguar. But it does have its good points." He presses a button on the door, and the seat between me and Diana flips up to reveal a mini bar. The only thing inside it is a bottle of champagne cradled in crushed ice.

"Starting the celebration early, eh?" I say. "Where are the glasses?"

"There's a compartment alongside the champagne. Open that up, and you'll find the flutes."

I hadn't noticed a hidden compartment there. But now that Hugh pointed it out, I find it easily and pop the lid to bring out four glasses. Then I hand the bottle to Hugh. "The groom should do the honors."

Diana turns away from the window. "Is it wise to pop a champagne cork inside a vehicle? What if it strikes one of us in the head or the eye or some other vulnerable spot?"

"No worries," Hugh says. "I know the safe method for doing this."

While he begins peeling the foil off the bottle's cap, I close the hidden compartment and scoot a little closer to Diana. I lean in to murmur, "Trust Hugh. He wouldn't put any of us in danger."

"I'm not afraid. But thank you for the reassurance."

"Why did you ask if it was safe if you aren't worried?"

"Hugh's assurance satisfied me."

She returns her attention to the view outside the window, so I scoot back over to my side of the bench.

Hugh has loosened the wire cage on the champagne bottle, but he doesn't remove it. I'm not an expert on how to open a bottle of champagne, but I have no doubts that Hugh is. He grasps the center of the bottle in one hand, then closes the other fist around the top and twists it. The cork comes out easily and stays caged in his hand.

"Nice work," I say. "I've never seen anybody do it that way."

"The flying cork method is the bourgeois way of opening a bottle. This is the aristocratic method."

Since he winks at me, I know he's just yanking my chain yet again.

"Maybe you know how to pop a champagne cork," I say, "but I'm the expert on how to pop the tab on a can of beer."

He scoffs. "Lord Sommerleigh does not stoop to guzzling beer."

"Really? Then your marriage won't last. Avery loves to swig some Budweiser now and then."

"I'm reeducating her in the proper way for Lady Sommerleigh to behave."

Hearing him use the title my sister will acquire on Saturday gives me a weird feeling in my gut. Avery, my baby sister, will become Lady

Sommerleigh. She'll be a titled aristocrat. Can I still call her Avery after that? Or will I be required to address her by her title? I've avoided thinking about that until now, but soon I'll have no choice.

Avery pours the champagne while Hugh holds the glasses for her. Then they hand one to me and one to Diana. She glances at me sideways again as she takes a dainty sip of the bubbly. Though she doesn't wince this time, she does flatten her lips.

She's uncomfortable riding in this car with me.

I swig a mouthful of champagne. The fizz burns down my throat, and I barely notice the flavor of the expensive beverage. I could buy a small car for the same cost as the champagne I'm currently drinking. Avery will become a wealthy woman in a matter of days, and though I shouldn't care about that, I can't help feeling like my sister won't have time for me anymore once she's married. I won't fit in with her new family. The Parrishes are nice people, but I'm not one of them.

Hugh and Avery seem to realize there's tension between me and Diana, and they do their best to lighten the mood with jokes and funny stories. I've already heard the tale of how Hugh and his best friend Callum nearly ruined their friendship by fighting over a woman, but I let him tell me all over again. Lord Sticky lost that battle. Callum got the girl, and Hugh got himself into major trouble in the aftermath.

Avery recounts how she met Hugh, but I've heard that story too. Diana also knows about that. Hugh slept with a woman who turned out to be a duke's wife and almost lost everything because of that one mistake. Rosalyn Parrish, Hugh's mother, stepped in to help her son by hiring my sister to refurbish Hugh's tarnished reputation. Avery succeeded, of course. She's the best image consultant anyone could hope to hire.

Now Hugh and Avery are getting married. On Saturday.

I sneak a surreptitious peek at Diana. She's smiling at a joke Hugh just told us, though I didn't pay attention to what he said. One thought keeps bouncing around in my brain. Do I have even a snowball's chance in hell of convincing Diana we could be a couple?

We pull over at a gas station, and the happy couple hops out of the limo to go "grab some goodies," as my sister says. Diana and I stay inside the car.

She looks at me.

I look at her.

Then she thrusts the door open and jumps out, racing into the gas station's store.

Do I have a snowball's chance? As Hugh would say, not bloody likely.

Chapter Twelve

Diana

A limousine ride through the countryside should be a relaxing experience, especially when we're drinking champagne during the trip. But sitting so close to Derek erases any relaxation I might have felt. This morning, we had sex in a janitorial closet in the building where we both work. Someone almost caught us. And heaven help me, that incident made me want us to get caught while still in the throes.

Have I become an exhibitionist? Perhaps I've simply been gagging for it after a long dry spell. Yes, that must be the reason I behaved like such a wanton. I still have my ruined knickers in my purse because I hadn't left the building since I arrived to work this morning.

The loo at the petrol station is far from luxurious, but I would've settled for a clean bathroom without amenities. This one is not shiny and clean. I make do, though, and relieve my immediate needs before browsing the snack offerings in the store. I've been ravenous all day, ever since the closet incident, and I crave the sort of foods that I rarely ever eat. But today, I grab every variety of junk food I can find, which requires the clerk behind the counter to fill up three plastic sacks.

By the time I return to the limo, Hugh and Avery are back inside the vehicle. Derek seems to have stayed put while the rest of us took care of whatever we needed to do. I doubt I'd want to know what the randy couple might have gotten up to in the store.

When I start to climb into the vehicle, Derek slides over to the other end of our bench so I won't need to crawl over him in order to sit down. He is a gentleman. And very considerate. An incredible lover too. No, not a lover. He's my donor and only my donor.

I'm getting bloody sick of reminding myself of that fact.

As I lay a hand on the seat, preparing to sit down, my foot slips and I stumble onto the bench, dropping my purse. Its flap falls open, exposing the lacy fabric of my ruined underwear. I snatch it up and awkwardly get in the correct position on the seat while managing to tug my dress back down from where it had ridden up my thigh.

Hugh and Avery are too engrossed in each other to have noticed.

I still have my sacks of snacks hung over my arm. As I set them on the bench beside me, I notice Derek watching me. His amused expression annoys me for some reason. So I hiss under my breath, "What are you smiling about?"

He speaks just as softly. "Kept a memento, hey?"

The blasted man thinks it's funny that I have my knickers in my purse. I couldn't very well toss them into the rubbish bin in my office.

"Memento of what?" Avery asks.

Her question stops me for one second too long.

Derek responds first. "Diana wanted to keep the champagne cork that you guys let fall onto the floor. It just fell out of her purse." He hands me the cork, though I have no idea why he'd been holding onto it. "Here you go. Something to remember today by."

I take the cork. But I know he was referring to when we had sex this morning, not the drive to Sommerleigh. I pray Avery and Hugh believe that story.

By the time we arrive at Sommerleigh House, I've eaten enough junk food to make an elephant nauseous, though it doesn't affect me that way. I love all that fattening, unhealthy, sinfully delicious rubbish. Only Pippa knew about my love for prepackaged snacks—until Derek came into my life. And now Hugh and Avery will learn my secret too.

But my biggest secret is the man sitting at the other end of the car bench.

The limousine parks in the gravel drive, directly in front of the steps that lead up to the doorway of the Sommerleigh House. Kendall, the butler, rushes out of the house to retrieve our luggage, rejecting the offers of Hugh and Derek who want to help the chap.

"No, sir, no," the butler insists. "You lot should go inside. I will bring you an aperitif to prepare your palates for dinner."

What a dedicated man that Kendall is. I have no servants, and I rather doubt Hugh likes having anyone at his beck and call. But he inherited Kendall, no doubt, and wouldn't want to put him out of a job.

The limo driver ends up helping Kendall, though I hear the butler trying to shoo the man away as we enter the house. Hugh leads us down the long hallway to the drawing room, where we take our seats to wait for Kendall to bring us our drinks. A few minutes later, Lady Sommerleigh walks into the room and sits down on the sofa beside her son and Avery. Rosalyn Parrish won't be Lady Sommerleigh anymore after Saturday, but we still address her by that title until then.

Kendall arrives a moment later, carrying a tray of drinks. "This is Dubonnet Rouge, a fortified wine. Enjoy your aperitifs, and I shall let you know as soon as dinner is ready."

I'm sure he added the explanation of what Dubonnet Rouge is strictly for Derek and Avery. They are, no doubt, unfamiliar with aperitifs.

Kendall discreetly bustles out of the room.

The wine is delicious, and dinner provides more than nourishment. It gives us all a chance to chat to each other and discuss how good the food is, and the happy couple inform us of the plans for the wedding and the festivities that will follow.

Since Hugh and Avery decided who would sit where during dinner, I find myself sandwiched between Derek and Lady Sommerleigh. Rosalyn is a lovely dinner companion. We've chatted a few times before, but I haven't visited Sommerleigh often and she rarely goes into the city. I'm closer to Rosalyn's age than to Derek's, though it hardly matters. We will never see each other again once I have that "bun in the oven," as Derek phrased it.

After dinner, we retire to the drawing room once again to partake of a digestif. I've never cared for after-dinner digestive drinks, and I doubt Hugh or Rosalyn do either, but I think they're trying to give their guests a memorable evening. I appreciate that, so I accept the digestif I'm offered—a glass of port. Not my favorite type of wine. But I can't deny the port the Parrishes have provided is much tastier than others I've had. They have excellent taste.

By the time the port is done and the conversation has waned, I'm yawning. The grandfather clock in the corner tells me it's now after ten o'clock. No wonder I'm sleepy. I rise at five a.m. every morning, but I woke even earlier today thanks to a filthy dream I had last night, a dream that involved Derek Hahn and a vat of whipped cream.

"I think Diana is ready for bed," Derek announces. "I'll escort the lady to her room."

Hugh winks at Derek. "Oh, yes. You definitely should take the lady to bed."

Avery elbows him in the side. "Behave, Hugh."

Rosalyn laughs. "That will never happen. Hugh was the naughtiest child in the entire Parrish family."

"That's a story I need to hear sometime," Derek says. "But not tonight."

I rise from my chair. "Rosalyn told me where my room is. I can find my own way, thank you."

"Not without your bodyguard." Derek approaches me and offers his arm. "Might as well give in. I know how to make a stubborn client do what I say."

A quick glance around the room confirms what I suspected. Everyone is watching us as if they think we are…a couple. I don't care what they think. So I march past Derek, pausing at the doorway. "Are you coming?"

"Yes, ma'am."

Derek follows a bit behind me until we reach the stairs to the upper floor. Then he cups his hand around my elbow as we ascend the steps. There really is no point in arguing with a stubborn man under these circumstances. Once I go into my room, he can't order me about anymore. We've just reached the landing when a commotion erupts downstairs, and I hear a familiar voice.

"Wow, this is amazing!" Pippa exclaims. "But where are Derek and Diana?"

"Up here," Derek shouts. "You missed dinner."

Pippa runs up the stairs and needs a moment to catch her breath. "We went to a restaurant for dinner and had all sorts of seafood that was soooo yummy."

"I'm glad you enjoyed yourself," I say. "But now it's bedtime."

"Can't sleep. I've had too much fun." Pippa yawns. "May I please watch TV with Sally? That's Rupert's daughter. Please?"

"You just yawned, pet. That means you need to go to bed."

Pippa's shoulders fall. "All right."

Derek slaps her arm. "Don't worry, kiddo. We've got all week to have bunches of fun. Better sack out now so you'll have the energy for all the great things we'll do tomorrow."

Pippa grins. "You're right. Where's my room?"

I have no idea, but before I can say that, Derek speaks up. "You're right next to Diana's room."

"And your room is on the other side of hers?" The girl sounds too pleased with that idea.

"That's right." He turns to me. "Let's show Pippa to her digs."

Derek leads the way since he somehow knows where our rooms are. But it's no mystery how he got that information. He is my bodyguard, so he would have discussed with Hugh and Rosalyn where everyone would sleep. And of course his room is adjacent to mine. It makes perfect sense and means nothing, other than that Derek excels at his job.

Pippa is thrilled when she sees her bags are already waiting for her in her room. Derek hovers just outside the doorway, out of our sight, while I make sure Pippa has settled in well enough. She begins to yawn more often, and I know she will fall asleep the second her head meets the pillow. So I shut the door behind me, but linger near the door until Pippa shuts off the light in her room.

Derek gestures toward my room. "You're next, Ms. Sangster."

"Please call me Diana this week as I've asked you to do before. We're on holiday, after all."

"*You* are. I'm still on duty."

"But this is your sister's wedding week." I open the door to my room but don't cross the threshold yet. "You shouldn't be working. I don't need protection here at Sommerleigh, so I order you to take the week off—and to call me Diana from this moment on, even after we go back to London."

"Okay. But only if you call me Derek."

"Agreed." I take two steps into the room, then face him. "Good night, Derek."

"Good night, Diana."

He saunters to the door of his room, winks at me, then disappears into his assigned quarters.

I shut my door and set about unpacking my clothes. Instead of a dresser, I discover I have a walk-in closet that isn't enormous but offers plenty of space for my belongings. Only after I've finished unpacking and changed into my night clothes do I notice what appears to be a doorway beside my bed. It must be a false door, or perhaps a remnant of a doorway that used to connect this room to the one next door. The most intriguing possibility is that the doorway leads into a secret passage.

I can't resist investigating the door, and I tiptoe up to the barrier to place a hand on the knob. Excitement ripples through me, which is a barmy response. But the idea that I might uncover some sort of secret drives me to press on, and I twist the knob carefully, slowly, all the while wondering what might lie beyond it.

The mystery is irresistible, so I pull the door open.

Derek stands on the other side, completely naked, facing me. He doesn't blink or move, his focus fastened to me.

And I enjoy a full-frontal view of his body. I'd known he had muscles hidden beneath the suits he always wears, but I had no idea how impressive his physique was. I know now. My eyes move of their own volition, taking in every inch of his body, from his thick biceps to his powerful thighs. But the part of him that seizes my focus hangs between his legs. I had gotten a glimpse of his cock twice, but now I can appreciate the full view of that beautiful dick, which seems to be swelling and thickening with every passing second.

"Diana," he snaps.

I blink rapidly and force myself to look at his face, though I feel somewhat dazed. It's ridiculous, but the sight of his nude body has short-circuited every neuron in my brain. And if he suggested we should get a leg over right now, I'd jump at the chance.

Chapter Thirteen

Derek

W hat?" Diana says, finally managing to speak after several seconds of staring at my body. Her lids flutter, and her lips have fallen open just a touch. Her tongue flicks out intermittently.

"If you keep staring at my dick, I'll need to drag you onto the bed and fuck you."

Do I want to do that? Hell yeah. Diana is the sexiest woman on the face of the earth. For reasons I can't figure out, she has spent months trying to convince herself she doesn't want me. It's bullshit, and I'm sure she realizes that. We want each other with a lust too powerful to deny. We've given in to it twice, and if I have my way, we'll give in many more times.

She's wearing sky blue PJs with puffy clouds on them, and even that turns me on.

"Why are you in the closet?" she asks, as her gaze wanders down to my dick and her tongue traces the outline of her lips, which have turned a darker shade of pink.

I can't help it. She looks so adorably confused that I chuckle while I stride up to the open doorway. "This isn't a closet, Diana. We have adjoining bedrooms."

"What? I don't understand."

I hook a finger under her chin and rub my thumb over her lips. "Adjoining bedrooms. That means this door connects our rooms. The happy couple arranged this, but I thought it was a good idea so I could stay close to watch over you, to do my job. But then you announced we should both just have fun this week." I skim my gaze over her, noting the way her nipples jut against the satin fabric of her PJs. "Didn't expect you to open the door."

Her gaze lands on my throat, which lies at her eye level. But her attention inexorably slides lower and lower, passing over my chest and belly until she reaches my groin. Yeah, I'm already getting an erection. Diana always does this to me.

I lift her chin. "Never would've imagined you would sleep in PJs, much less ones that have puffy clouds on them. I like it."

"Pippa gave them to me."

"Ah, of course. That explains it." I bend my head closer to hers, and our breaths reflect off each other. "You're a good mom to that kiddo. You absolutely should have a baby."

"But I work too much."

"You're a smart woman, and you'll work out the logistics."

She glances at my dick again, swallows hard enough that I can see the movement, then straps her arms over her chest. After a few seconds, she finally lifts her gaze to mine. "Good night, Derek."

Diana reaches for the doorknob.

I lay my hand over hers. "Wait a minute. There's something I think we really need to do."

"Right now? I'm knackered."

"This will only take a minute." I tuck a lock of hair behind her ear. "We've had sex twice, but we've only kissed once. Let's do it one more time."

"Why? Kissing is irrelevant to our deal."

"Come on, Diana, you liked it the first time. Now that we've gotten physical together, wouldn't you like to know whether kissing will feel different now?"

"It doesn't matter."

"Please, Diana." I'm pleading for a woman to kiss me. Never would have imagined I'd behave this way, but the more time I spend with her, the more I want this thing between us to be more than sex.

She squares her shoulders and lifts her chin. "No kissing. That's my final word on the matter."

Diana Sangster shuts the door in my face.

Well, at least she didn't slam it.

I drop onto the bed and try to sleep, which is damn difficult when I've got a raging erection. But I pull off the feat by picturing slabs of raw meat dripping with blood. Yeah, it's morbid and gruesome. But the tactic works, and I finally fall asleep.

At seven a.m., someone bangs on my door.

I groan as I crawl out of bed. When that someone bangs on the door again, I holler, "Hold your horses, would you? I'll be there in a sec."

"Breakfast will be served in fifteen minutes, Derek," Avery says. "Don't be late."

"I didn't know we had a strict schedule for meals." I pull on my slacks, the ones I'd worn yesterday with my suit, and hustle over there to open the door before Avery can decide to barge right in. "Isn't this supposed to be a vacation?"

"Yes, but we still have an itinerary." She pats my cheek. "Don't worry. We've penciled in plenty of free time."

"Penciling that in doesn't sound relaxing. Have you also jotted down the times when I'm allowed to hit the head?"

"Don't be silly. Your bathroom breaks are your business. I wouldn't pencil that in."

I wipe a hand across my forehead. "Whew. For a minute there, I thought I might need to call for a shrink to work out your OCD."

"Ha-ha. Get dressed and meet us in the solarium. Kendall has set up a buffet table for us."

"I'll be there on time. Should I pinky swear?"

My sister rolls her eyes and walks away.

After a quick shower and shave, I pull on my casual clothes. Luckily, I'd brought plenty of that kind of stuff, since I assumed I wouldn't dress in my usual suits and ties this week even if I kept up my bodyguard duties. By the time I step into the solarium, everybody else is already there. Chairs and small tables have been set up around the room, and the buffet table is tucked against one wall. The side of the room that faces the garden consists of wall-to-wall glass panes. Just outside those windows lies a patio, and I can see the sprawling garden nearby. The glass doors have been thrown wide open, but nobody is sitting at the patio table.

Sommerleigh is a beautiful estate. The Parrishes take good care of it, and I've always admired the way they keep up the traditional look of the house and grounds, rather than updating it to a more modern style.

The buffet table holds more than enough food to feed this group. Rupert's wife arrived late last night and brought their son with her. Pippa sits at a small table with Rupert's daughter Sally, while Rupert and his wife occupy a nearby table along with their son. A longer table accommodates Rosalyn, Hugh, Avery, and Diana with one empty place—set for me, I'm sure.

Naturally, the empty chair is right next to Diana. Avery arranged this. I have no doubts about that. But I suspect Hugh conspired with her. If they think seating me next to Diana at breakfast will make her fall in love with me, they're delusional. She wouldn't even let me kiss her last night.

Am I giving up on her? No. But I need to adjust my plans to win her over. Diana is one tough cookie, but I'll find a way to make her crumble in my hands.

Now I'm using cookie metaphors. Better not do that out loud. It's no way to seduce a woman.

We have a normal meal for a while, grabbing what we want from the buffet and chatting while we eat. I wind up talking to Rosalyn most of the time, while Diana talks to Hugh and Avery. When my sister sneakily suggests that we should change places to make sure everybody gets to talk to everyone else, it doesn't quite turn out the way she must've hoped.

Diana moves over to Rupert's table and gets to know him and his wife.

I go hang out with the kids, who have moved out onto the patio with their food. When I glance back at the solarium, Avery is standing in the open doorway, hands on her hips, lips puckered. Oh yeah, she's annoyed. At me. I screwed up her meddling scheme, though it wasn't all my fault. She decided to switch things up and failed to specify what exactly that meant.

Yeah, okay, I would rather have stayed with Diana. But once I realized my sister planned to use this breakfast buffet as a tool for meddling, I knew I needed to jam a monkey wrench into her scheme before Diana noticed what was happening. She wouldn't have liked that at all.

Seducing Diana Sangster will take finesse and patience. Avery doesn't get that.

Once breakfast is over, we all go our separate ways. This is some of the downtime Avery penciled in for us. We have one hour to ourselves, then the games begin. Avery wouldn't tell me what type of games she and Hugh have planned, only that it's "the outdoors kind" and it will be "a hoot and a half."

"What is half a hoot?" I had asked.

My sister just rolled her eyes.

Now, I'm wandering around inside Sommerleigh House, trying to find the woman I want to seduce. When the gang left the solarium, Avery had immediately cornered me to share the morning's itinerary, and I didn't see which way Diana had gone.

"Looking for your girl?"

I'd been leaning through the drawing-room door, but Hugh's voice makes me turn around to face him. "I don't have a girl, Lord Sticky."

"You'll never win her heart if you deny your feelings for her."

"Since when do we chat about women? That's not our thing. We lob insults at each other."

Hugh sighs with plenty of sarcasm. "Yes, you're right. I've spent too many hours listening to women discuss wedding plans. I've learned that pink is not pink, it's salmon. And green is not green after all, it's asparagus."

"You're totally whipped now, aren't you? Avery has you wrapped around her pinky finger." I sling an arm around his shoulders. "Better do something macho and do it quick. Maybe your best friend will bring some cabers with him."

"I doubt those will fit in Callum's car."

"Wanna have a fist fight?"

Hugh chuckles. "No, but thank you for the offer."

I step away from him. "Were you looking for me for a reason?"

"Bollocks! Yes, I almost forgot. Avery insisted I needed to let you know Diana is in the garden, alone." He holds up his hands, palms out. "I am merely the messenger."

"Yeah, I know. Avery is going nuts with the matchmaking."

Avery pops her head out of a doorway at the far end of the hall. "Hugh, hurry up. I need your input."

I lean in to whisper to Hugh, "If she asks what color you like, say chartreuse."

"Why?"

"To shut her up. I doubt she knows what color that is. Nobody does."

He nods. "Ah, I see."

Lord Sommerleigh trots down the hall, and I head outside to find Diana.

I finally track her down on the far side of the garden, well away from the house, just as she's turning down the dirt path that leads to the summer house. I would call it a gazebo, but I'm not British.

"Wait up, Diana," I call out to her.

She stops and turns halfway toward me. Her brows wrinkle. "What are you doing?"

"Coming to find you."

"Why?"

"Because I wanted to see you." I move closer, leaving an arm's length between us. "I think we should talk."

"About what? If you've changed your mind about our deal—"

"I haven't. But I'd like to get to know you better."

"Why?"

She seems honestly confused by my statement. I knew I'd be facing an uphill battle to get her to open up and talk to me, like adults having a normal conversation, but I hadn't expected this steep a slope ahead of me. Do I want this enough to fight for her? Yeah, I do.

"Let's go to the summer house," I say. "It's a private spot where we can talk about everything. Is that such a bad thing?"

"No, I suppose not."

"Then you'll come with me?"

She wraps her arms around herself. "Yes, I will."

We walk side by side down the dirt path until we reach the summer house, then ascend the steps. Inside the structure, benches built into walls offer a place to sit. I settle onto a bench and expect Diana will choose a spot further away from me. Instead, she sits beside me with only a foot separating us.

"This is a beautiful spot," I say. "But why did you want to come here alone?"

She stares up at the roof for a moment, then looks at me. "I needed to think. With Pippa coming home, I have to reconsider what I want to do."

"About what?"

"Everything."

I think I finally get why she needed to find a solitary place and why Avery wanted me to know Diana had come out here alone. This time, I don't think it's meddling. Avery probably assumes I can make Diana feel better or at least get her to tell me what's wrong. My sister might be overestimating how much Diana trusts me.

But I'm about to find out either way.

Chapter Fourteen

Diana

When I'd woken this morning, I'd felt as if a weight had been lifted off my chest and I could breathe again. My only regret was that I hadn't let Derek kiss me last night, and I spent most of today wondering if I should tell him I do want that. Our kiss a few days ago had affected me more than I wanted to admit. But the more time I spend with Derek, the better I feel about…everything.

Until an hour ago. My hopes had evaporated in an instant.

"You can tell me what's wrong," Derek says. "I'm a good listener. Just ask Rosalyn and Avery. Even Hugh would vouch for me."

"I don't need references. You've been guarding me for three months, which means I trust you already."

"Okay. Does that mean you'll tell me why you seem so sad right now?" He moves his hand as if to hold mine but pulls it away. "You had a good time at breakfast. Didn't you?"

"Yes, I did."

"What changed?"

I don't normally discuss private matters, especially the sort that's bothering me now. I feel completely deflated, but I can't tell Derek why. Not directly. Since I know he won't give up until I give him a crumb of a reason, I'll need to be vague about it. "I'm feeling off right now, that's all."

"Off? Are you sick?"

"No." I wring my hands, which I have never done in my life, and I can't look at him. "It's a womanly issue. A man wouldn't understand."

"I grew up with a younger sister. You'd be surprised what I understand about 'womanly' things."

Why must he be so obstinate? Any other man would have given up after I mentioned my "womanly issue." For heaven's sake, I don't want to discuss this with Derek Hahn. But he's being so sweet and understanding that I can't simply tell him to bugger off.

I squeeze my eyes shut and say, "I'm having my period."

Silence. Leaves rustle high up in the trees, but I hear no other sound, certainly nothing from Derek.

Until he laughs softly. "Did you think that would horrify me? Told you, I have a sister. Couldn't help overhearing our mom telling Avery how to use those pads."

I peel my lids apart. "You don't understand. This means I'm not pregnant."

"Diana, I'm not stupid. I know that's what it means. But why does that upset you so much?"

"Because it means we can't have sex for four days, and then I probably won't be fertile again for a week or two." I let my head fall back against the post behind me. "I wanted to get this over with as soon as possible."

"Get what over with?"

"Our arrangement. I want to get it over with, so we won't need to shag ever again."

He falls silent, and I glance at him. Derek has his jaw firmly set, his hands fisted on his thighs, and his lips compressed. He seems to have a hard glint in his eyes too.

"What's wrong?" I ask.

He stares at me for a moment, his entire body strung as taut as a high-tension wire. "What's wrong? Are you kidding me? You just announced that you want to get it over with so you can send me away to America and never see me again."

I have no idea how to respond to that statement, and I need a moment to digest what it means. He can't be implying… No, he doesn't want to have a relationship with me. Derek agreed to my terms and assured me he understood them. He has no right to have hurt feelings now.

"Of course I want to get it over with," I say. "Casual sex makes me feel unclean afterward."

"So now screwing me is a sin. Didn't sound that way when we were fucking and you were screaming because you came so hard."

My spine snaps ramrod straight, and I seem to have lost control of my own vocal cords. Nothing else explains why I say, "This deal was a bloody stupid idea. I should never have suggested it. You were right, we should use the turkey baster method."

He glares at me for so long that my skin starts to itch from the intensity of his focus on me. Then he shuts his eyes, his shoulders wilt, and he releases the weariest sigh I've ever heard. "If that's how you really feel…"

Derek rises and clomps down the steps to stalk off down the path to the garden. I sit here immobilized until I can no longer see him. Then I rest my elbows on my knees and cradle my head in my raised hands. Perhaps I should tell him the real reason I can't offer him anything more than what our deal allows. But sharing that with him would mean we are…involved in some fashion.

I cannot go down that road again.

After a few more minutes, I walk back to the house and check every room, but don't find a soul inside the house, at least on the first floor. Even the kitchen is empty. As I set a hand on the banister, ready to mount the stairs to the second floor, the front door swings open.

Kendall trots up to me, leaving the door ajar. "Ms. Sangster, there you are. Lady Sommerleigh requests that you join us on the lawn for a game of cricket."

"I don't play sports."

"Lord Sommerleigh would also like for you to join them, even if you don't play."

This is Hugh and Avery's wedding week. It would be rude to refuse the invitation. "Yes, I'll join the others."

Kendall insists on walking me out of the house and onto the large mowed lawn, where everyone has gathered and a cricket pitch has been created on the grass. I thank Kendall for accompanying me, and he gives me a crisp nod, then trots back into the house.

Chairs have been set up along this side of the lawn, so everyone who is not participating in the match can watch in comfort. I have never enjoyed sports of any kind, but especially not cricket. It's the most boring game. But I will pretend to care who does the best job of whacking the ball, and I will pretend to give a toss about who wins. Every man on the pitch is a friend of mine. I can't reasonably be expected to choose a side.

Off to my left, well away from the adults, I see Pippa and the other children sitting at the patio table playing some sort of board game.

"Glad you could join us," Hugh shouts while waving at me.

"You don't have enough players for a match."

"No, but this is just for fun today. The real match will be tomorrow, after the reinforcements have arrived."

Hugh turns his attention to Derek and Rupert, the only other men on the lawn. They seem to be having a serious discussion, probably about how to play cricket with only three men. They're wearing everyday clothes rather than official cricket gear.

"Come sit with me, Diana."

Avery is sitting on a lawn chaise with a drink in her hand. She pats the chaise beside hers.

I accept her invitation and settle onto the seat. "Is that a rhubarb cordial you're drinking?"

"Yes. Kendall suggested it, and that man is always right about drinks and food." Avery takes a sip. "Mm, this is super yummy. I got one for you too."

She reaches under her chaise and brings out another glass.

I take the drink and sip it. "Yes, it is lovely. The best rhubarb cordial I've ever had."

"Why do you think Rosalyn keeps Kendall around? He's a treasure."

As I take another sip, my gaze wanders to the lawn and the men gathered there. Derek glances this way but studiously avoids looking at me. I can't blame him. Our argument left me feeling uneasy, and he was quite angry about what I said. Though I feel a strong urge to apologize to him, I won't do that. We have a deal. He shouldn't get angry because I reminded him of the parameters.

My skin starts to itch again. *Bloody hell.*

I do not feel bad about what happened. I don't.

Derek finally aims his gaze at me—and scowls. Then he grabs a cricket bat and starts swinging it around as if he means to whack an invisible ball. Hugh says something to him, and Derek bows his head, no longer swinging his bat wildly. He nods twice. Hugh pats his arm.

Derek needs consoling? No, it must have been something else. Hugh might have been explaining the rules of the game to Derek. Oh yes, that makes perfect sense.

"Something happened," Avery says. "Between you and Derek. He's upset."

"We had a minor disagreement. It's nothing. You know how sensitive men can be."

"Not Derek. He's rock solid."

She loves her brother, so of course she views him as rock solid. It's my fault he isn't behaving that way now. I raise my glass and down half the contents. And then I start coughing. I lean forward, but that does not help.

Avery slaps my back several times until I've stopped coughing. "Better?"

"Yes, thank you." My hoarse voice belies that assertion, but Avery has the good sense not to press me for an explanation. "I think I'll go back into the house. It's rather warm for me out here."

That's rubbish, but Avery accepts my excuse.

I go upstairs to my room, but then I can't remember why I came up here. To escape, that's why. I've made a ruddy mess of everything, and I don't know why I've done that. Well, I might have a clue. But every time I try to think about that, my mind rebels and spurs me to say and do things I shouldn't.

Someone knocks on the bedroom door.

I can't move.

That person knocks again. "Diana? Are you in there?"

Bugger me. It's Derek. If I say nothing, maybe he will go away. Now I'm acting like a schoolgirl. That man drives me insane. But I refuse to behave like a spoiled child, so I march up to door and pull it open.

"There you are," he says. "Avery told me you came inside. Are you feeling okay?"

"Yes. Why wouldn't I be?"

"Avery also said you guzzled an entire glass of something called a rhubarb cordial."

"It's non-alcoholic."

He leans against the jamb. "Good. Then we can finish that conversation now, since you aren't hammered."

"Not here."

"Why not?"

I have no reasonable response to that query. We've had sex, which means I shouldn't be embarrassed to invite him into my room. Derek is too much of a gentleman to seduce me after our argument earlier.

"Come in," I say, as I step aside to let him pass. Then I shut the door again. "Sit wherever you like."

This bedroom is large and has two chairs as well as a small sofa, not to mention a sizable bed.

Derek takes one of the chairs.

I perch on the bed's edge, at the foot.

"What happened earlier…" He trails off as he rubs his hands on his thighs. "I'm sorry I got annoyed about what you said. It won't happen again."

"You should be annoyed. I said things I wish I hadn't." I wince. "Such as the suggestion that we should use a turkey baster."

"I wasn't offended by that." He leans back in his chair, his posture more relaxed. "But it's a lot more fun to make a donation my way."

"Yes, it is."

"Did you just agree with me?"

I fold my arms over my chest. "We both agreed to do this your way. Of course I concur with what you said."

He looks down at the floor and scratches his jaw. "I should explain why I reacted that way. Getting annoyed, I mean."

"You owe me no explanations."

"But you need to understand." He pushes up out of the chair and stands at the window, gazing out at the sky or perhaps the lawn. "You see, I feel—"

A series of crisp knocks rattle the door. "Pippa wants you on the lawn, Diana."

That is Rupert's voice.

I hurry to the door and yank it open. "Is Pippa injured?"

"No, nothing like that. She wants you to be there for her first attempt at playing cricket."

"Oh, I see." I glance back at Derek. "Would you care to join us?"

He sighs. "Sure."

As the three of us head out to the lawn, I wonder what Derek had been about to tell me. "I feel," he'd said. But Rupert interrupted whatever else he might have spoken if he had the chance. Even while I watch Pippa learn to play cricket, I can't stop wondering.

What does Derek feel?

Chapter Fifteen

Derek

I'm not sure if I should be glad Rupert interrupted us or if I should smack him upside the head. He couldn't know he'd walked in on a serious conversation. Hell, Diana probably didn't realize that either. I started to say "I feel," but I didn't get to finish the sentence. What had I wanted to tell her?

I feel something for you, Diana, something more than lust.

It's probably for the best that she never heard me speak those words. She insists she only wants me for sex, and only until she's pregnant. That won't happen this week. Maybe that gives me some time to ease her into the concept of a real relationship. Back in Diana's bedroom, I'd wanted to tell her a lot more than that.

Out on the lawn, everybody watches Hugh giving Pippa a lesson on how to rock cricket. I'd always thought of cricket as an old person's game, but I must've been confusing it with something else because this is not an easygoing enterprise. No, it's more like a cross between baseball and football—the American version of football. Don't even get me started on the sport Brits call football, and that Americans know is really soccer.

Hugh and I have argued often about whose version of football is the real one. That's how guys bond. Since Hugh is about to become my brother-in-law, I figured we needed to harass each other relentlessly to prove we can survive being in-laws.

I've got the best seat in the house—or the lawn, technically—for watching Pippa learn about cricket. Avery sits on my left, while Diana is on my right. We're all too engrossed in Hugh's attempt to train a teenage girl to talk to each other. But I can't resist razzing the coach.

I cup my hands like a megaphone and holler, "Are you sure you've played this game before, Hugh? Looks to me like Pippa's schooling you."

The teenager flashes me a grin.

Hugh swings his bat in a circle, then thumps its tip on the ground. "I was playing cricket before you learned how to drive a car. Oh, wait. You still haven't mastered that skill, have you?"

"I stole your keys, Lord Sticky. I'll be doing donuts around the driveway in your Jag while you're getting pointers from a kid. I'll make sure to drive really fast so all that pea gravel will scratch up your baby."

"Yes, you are so bloody terrifying." Hugh thumps his bat on his palm. "Maybe you and I should have a private match."

"Anytime, Lord Sticky, anytime."

My sister leans over to whisper to me, "Hugh is really good at cricket. You don't even know the rules."

"How hard can it be? I played football in high school, and I studied mixed martial arts to get ready for becoming a bodyguard."

Avery looks past me to Diana. "Would you tell him? He won't listen to me."

"Why do you think Derek will listen to me?" Diana asks. "Men are impossible. They would rather beat each other senseless than resolve their issues in a dignified manner."

I groan. "Come on, ladies. Hugh and I don't actually want to beat each other up. But I would like to learn to play cricket just so I can whup Hugh's ass. Gotta hold up the American end."

Diana glances at my ass.

And my sister smirks.

Women. No man understands them, and trying to unlock their mysteries will drive a guy insane. Despite their cockamamie ideas, I love the ladies. Especially the two seated on either side of me.

Hugh goes back to teaching Pippa about cricket, and we all watch the kid getting better and better at the game. She's picking up on it so fast that I bet she'll be whupping the adults in no time.

Just as Hugh and Pippa are wrapping up their coaching session, several cars come up the driveway. I recognize most of those vehicles because they belong to Hugh's buddies, the Brits who all married Americans. The Dixons and Hunters have arrived, and I think I see the Mithorian delegation too. That would be the royal family from the island principality of Mithoria. Bennett Montague and his wife Samantha had RSVP'd for the wedding, and they had asked if their families could come too.

Avery and Hugh said yes, naturally. Once the Scots contingent arrives, Sommerleigh will be stuffed to the gills. Since the house doesn't have enough rooms for everyone, most of the guests volunteered to find accommodation in one of the nearby villages.

Hugh and Rupert rush over to the driveway to instruct the wedding guests where to park their cars. Sommerleigh features a massive garage, so the guests who staying here will stow their rides in that building. Others are directed toward the far end of the lawn, right beside the garage.

How are all these people going to fit inside the dining room this evening? We can have lunch alfresco, but dinner is a more formal event for the Parrishes.

The rest of the day passes in a blur. I have so many conversations with so many people that I lose track of who I told what, never mind what they might've said to me. Still, it's a lot of fun. Catching up with everyone is great, but I'd like to find some time to be alone with Diana, though it's unlikely I'll get that today. Everybody's excited about the wedding.

We do have lunch outside, and I don't know how the kitchen staff can keep up with cooking and serving all the food, but they pull it off. The guests start out on the patio, then spill over onto the lawn as they split off into smaller groups.

After lunch, I need a break from all this revelry. So I sneak away to the summer house.

The garden insulates this spot from the house and the guests having a party on the lawn, giving me a nice quiet place to kick back and relax. I lie down on the bench inside the summer house, linking my hands under my head, and close my eyes. The only sounds I hear are birds chirping.

Ahhh, this is perfect.

Footsteps draw closer.

Oh, no. I was into the solitude, but now somebody probably wants to drag me back to the big hoedown. I push myself up into a sitting position and set my feet on the floor. I still have my eyes closed as I yawn and stretch.

"Did I disturb you?"

My lids fly open, and my gaze veers to Diana. She stands on the top step of the summer house. My pulse speeds up. "Hey, Diana."

She shuffles a little closer. "Mind if I join you?"

"It's a free bench. Come on over."

Diana settles in beside me. Right beside me. Her leg brushes against mine. She clasps her hands on her lap. "You wanted to say something this morning."

"Yeah, I did."

"Would you tell me now?"

I fidget on the bench. It's dumb, but I feel anxious about telling her the truth. "Maybe we should talk about it another time. Today has been a whirlwind, and we're both wiped out."

"Yes, it has been quite a day." She studies me for a moment. "I'm only a guest for the wedding, but your sister is getting married. That must be stressful for you, especially since your mother and father passed away years ago. Avery told me about that."

"Women gab about everything, don't you?"

"I like Avery. We've become friends, and I'm sure that's why she felt comfortable sharing something from her past with me."

"She hasn't had many friends. Her job used to take her around the world, so she was always too busy to have a social life. All of that changed when she met Hugh." I move my hand toward Diana's leg, instinctively wanting to hold her hand, but I stop short of doing it. I doubt she would want that. "I'm happy for Avery and Hugh, but the wedding stuff has made me reflect on my life. I've never been married or engaged. Had serious girlfriends, but those relationships always fizzled out. Maybe I'm the problem."

Why the hell did I just spill my guts to Diana? I must be "barmy," as the Brits would say. Or maybe I'm a "bampot," as the Scots would say.

Diana stares blankly at me for several seconds. Then she clasps my hand. "I've had similar troubles with men, though I was married once."

"Seriously? Nobody mentioned that."

"Why would they? It was a long time ago, and I haven't talked about that with anyone since the divorce."

She chose to tell me, after keeping it to herself for years. I want to know more about her marriage, but I can't decide if I should ask any questions. Though I've never been afraid to speak my mind, this is the first time in my life that I've found a woman who makes me feel like we could have something that lasts more than a while, something that lasts forever.

Yeah, I'm barmy for sure.

Diana squeezes my hand. "You are not the problem. Those women must have been idiots to let you get away."

"Uh, thanks. It's weird to hear you say that since you only want my body." Time to man up and just say it. "I want more than that with you, Diana. A lot more."

She doesn't rip her hand away like I'd expected. She doesn't seem horrified either. "You are the first man who ever made me wish I were capable of more, of what you want from me. But my marriage changed me, and I can't erase those scars."

"Maybe you can't erase them, but scars can heal."

Diana releases my hand, folding hers on her lap as she gazes down at them. "Has Pippa told you how she came to be in my care?"

"No. I've wondered, but it's not my place to ask. You never mentioned having a ward when you hired my company to protect you."

"Pippa is not my ward. Legally, she is my daughter. I adopted her after her father died. He was my younger brother." She bows her head and says nothing for a moment. "Fifteen years ago, Roger met and impulsively married a woman who had a history of addiction. He desperately wanted to help her recover from that, and she did try, but only while she was pregnant with Pippa. Once the baby was born, Amanda ran away. Roger eventually found her. She had died of an overdose."

"That's awful. But something must've happened to Roger too."

Diana nods and finally lifts her head to look at me. "Six years ago, he was killed in an airline crash. In his will, he named me as

Pippa's guardian. I've loved that girl since the day she was born and helped care for her while Roger tried to work things out with Amanda. Now Pippa is legally my daughter."

"Why didn't you want anybody to know about Pippa? I got the impression Avery and Hugh didn't even know."

"I prefer to keep my private life private." She sags against the summer house wall. "Pippa wants to call me Mum, but I've resisted that."

"That kid loves you to pieces. Why wouldn't you let her call you Mom?"

She shrugs one shoulder. "I suppose I don't feel worthy of it. I kept Pippa at home, and in public school as Roger had wanted, until three months ago. Then I sent her away. I've always worked too hard and not spent enough time with her. I don't deserve to be her mother."

"Pippa is a terrific kid. Smart too. And she adores you. Stop being so hard on yourself." I brush the backs of my fingers over her cheek. "But yeah, you do work too much. You need to cut yourself some slack, Diana. We all do the best we can."

Our gazes connect, and for a moment, we just look into each other's eyes. Then she rests her head on my shoulder. "Would you tell me about your longest relationship?"

"Sure. It lasted fourteen months. Eventually, I found out that Wendy had been cheating on me for the whole time. She said I just wasn't enough for her, since I was working too much and not paying enough attention to her needs." To have Diana's head on my shoulder feels right somehow, and any anxiety I might've had melts away. "When we broke up, Wendy filed a palimony suit and tried to take me for every penny I had. But in my work as a bodyguard, I'd gotten to know a few private investigators. I hired one and got the proof that Wendy had cheated repeatedly. The suit was dismissed, but I was shell-shocked after that."

I swear I feel an actual weight lifting off me just from sharing my past with Diana. Something important just happened between us. But is it enough to change her mind about us?

Chapter Sixteen

Diana

I can't believe any woman would throw you over that way," I tell Derek. "She must have been a bloody moron. You are the most loyal, compassionate man I've ever met, and any woman with half a brain would snap you up in an instant."

He chuckles. "That means you should snap me up, hey? You have a whole brain, after all, not just half of one. But don't worry. I'm not expecting you to throw yourself at me. I appreciate the compliment, though."

"It's well deserved."

Can't believe I told him about my past, but I'm not sorry I did. He shared his past too, which makes me feel things I can't quite describe. Not bad things.

"Do you still want to do the baby pact thing?" he asks. "I'll understand if you'd rather go to one of those banks or a clinic."

Perhaps I should terminate our deal. But I don't want to do that. Is this still about having a baby? Or has it morphed into something altogether different?

"Our deal is still in force," I say. "Unless you've changed your mind."

"I haven't."

As we sit here listening to the birds that sing high up in the trees, I suddenly realize how one-sided our agreement is. I haven't offered him anything of real value in return, only the chance to move back to America and work for a celebrity. If I'm completely honest with myself, I know I presented that opportunity to him because I'm afraid that I might develop feelings for him. Maybe I already have. But I still can't quite commit to anything more than sex.

"I haven't told you about my marriage," I say. "You talked about your longest relationship, so I feel I should discuss mine with you."

"Only if you want to. I don't expect you to tell me everything about yourself."

"But I'd like to explain. It might help you understand why I am this way."

He raises his brows. "What way are you?"

"Uptight and demanding."

"That's now how I would describe you."

I shouldn't ask, but I can't stop myself. "How would you describe me?"

"Smart, strong, tough when it's necessary, determined, caring... Should I keep going? It would take an entire thesaurus to list all your amazing qualities."

I freeze, and even my eyelids won't move.

He glides one finger down my cheek. "Don't look so shocked. You only need to look at Pippa to see the proof of how incredible you are. She's a special girl, and that's all down to you."

"No, I—"

"Yes, it's true. Ask Pippa sometime. She'll tell you."

My cheeks feel a touch warm. I need to change the subject, and I did offer to tell him my story. "I was married to Lyle for fifteen years. We met at university and married a year later. Our marriage went smoothly at first, until we both graduated and secured good jobs at the firms we'd wanted to work for. We both had studied business, but I began to achieve success rather quickly while he struggled to find his place. It caused...strife between us."

"I've known people who had the same issues. But I'm guessing there's more to the story."

"Yes." I rub my palms on my trousers because they've suddenly turned clammy. No one has ever heard this story, except for my brother—and he would have kept the secret no matter what. But now, I need to tell Derek about it. "The more successful I became, the more withdrawn and sullen Lyle became. He started to drink, moderately at first, but then more heavily. Back then, I believed a couple should stay together and work through their issues no matter how long it took. But Lyle… He changed."

My throat feels tight, and I must seem anxious because Derek takes both my hands and surrounds them with his larger ones. The warmth of his touch gives me the strength to tell the rest of my story.

"Lyle stopped drinking," I say, "when his employer threatened to fire him if he didn't clean up his act. He did that. And to his credit, he never drank again. But he grew to resent me even more as the years went by, so much that he belittled me at every turn. And I let him, because I felt guilty for having success when he didn't."

"I'm guessing something went seriously wrong between you two."

I shut my eyes as the memories assail me. "Lyle sneaked into my office one day and photocopied sensitive client files. He then released them to the media. I was sacked for not having secured my files well enough. Lyle simply wanted to humiliate me. I filed for divorce the very next day."

"Shit, that's awful. I hope you reamed that bastard in the courtroom."

"Thankfully, I hadn't become wealthy yet at that point. Lyle received half of our assets, but that didn't amount to as much as he would've liked to get, and it didn't bankrupt me. But I spent years repairing the damage to my career and my self-esteem. Not sure I ever succeeded with the latter."

Derek gives my hand a light squeeze. "You succeeded in every way, Diana. You became a billionaire, and you've helped tons of people start up their own businesses. You've raised Pippa too."

"Yes, but I gave up my own happiness to achieve that success in business. I could've been a better caregiver to Pippa too."

"Sounds to me like you're still letting your ex mess with your head. You have a great life with Pippa, don't you?"

I nod. "But I could have done better with her."

"That's not what she says." He rotates toward me, still clasping my hands. "We both have bad things in the past that changed us and that still haunt us. But we can choose to move past that stuff. We can choose to be happy."

His words, the tone of his voice, and the look on his face affect me so deeply that the start of tears burn in my eyes. Derek means every word of what he said. Can we simply choose to be happy? To move on from the past and create a better future? Perhaps we can. But the most frightening question of all looms between us.

Do we want to craft that future together?

My mobile rings.

I pull my hands free of his and answer the call—because it's Pippa ringing me. "Yes, pet, what is it?"

"Dinner will be served in twenty minutes. Kendall just told us. Where are you?"

"In the summer house."

"All alone?" Pippa sounds disgusted by that thought.

"No, dear, I am not alone. Derek is with me."

"Brilliant! Are you two kissing?"

A laugh splutters out of me. "No, of course not. Honestly, you do say the most outrageous things sometimes. We will be there for dinner. Goodbye, Pippa."

I disconnect the call before she can say anything else that's utterly ludicrous. Kissing in the summer house? Derek and I have only kissed once, but Pippa knows nothing about that. She has fairytale fantasies about what adult relationships are like.

Derek rests an arm on the bench behind me. "What outrageous thing did Pippa say?"

"It was nothing."

"You laughed, and saliva went spraying everywhere. Must've been a doozy, whatever she said to you."

I suppose I might as well tell him. "She asked if we were kissing."

His lips curve up gradually until they form a sly smile. "That's a provocative question, eh?"

"Pippa has odd ideas about what you and I do together."

He compresses his lips, and his whole body starts to quiver as if he's struggling not laugh at me. "Odd ideas, huh? Good thing she's too young and innocent to guess what we really get up to."

"She will never know."

"Until she starts dating."

That might be the most horrifying idea I've heard. I suppose every mother wants her child to stay innocent forever, but they always grow up and learn the joys of kissing—and sex. I pray Pippa won't rush into the physical side of romance.

"Where are your parents?" Derek asks. "You haven't mentioned them."

"They moved to Canada shortly after I married Lyle."

"So, if they're still around, why did your brother make you Pippa's guardian?"

"My parents were older than average when they had children. They were in their seventies when Roger passed away, and he hadn't wanted Mum and Dad to endure the stress of living with a precocious young girl."

Derek's expression grows tight, as if he once again can't decide whether to ask a question. But he blows out a breath and asks. "Why did your parents move so far away? I would've thought they'd want to stick around and get to see Pippa grow up."

"They were devastated after Roger's death. I think they simply couldn't deal with the loss, not at the time. Pippa and I have visited them a few times. I was never particularly close with my parents."

"That's too bad." Derek sits up straighter and slaps his hands on his thighs. "Okay, enough serious talk. It's time to make out."

"What?" The word comes out as half question, half laughter. "I did not suggest we should do that."

"No, but I'm suggesting it." He slings an arm around my waist and pulls me close. "Let's make out, Diana. We have time before we go to dinner."

"The sun is setting."

"Perfect. A romantic atmosphere for our second kiss."

I should remind him this is not a romance, but I don't want to do that. Something has changed between us, and I realize that I do want Derek to kiss me. Deeply. Sensually. Until I dissolve into him. Only Derek Hahn has ever turned me into a warm puddle of desire.

"Yes," I murmur. "Kiss me, please."

He slides a hand into my hair, cradling my head, and presses his mouth to mine. His tongue flicks out to tease my lips, and I do dissolve into him, feeling so warm and liquid that I know I would fall to the ground if he pulled his arm away from me. The woodsy scent of his cologne tantalizes my senses while he teases me with brief, slow kisses until I grow slick and achy between my thighs. When he wraps both arms around me and thrusts his tongue between my lips, my rigid nipples scrape against the fabric of my shirt and I moan.

Derek deepens the kiss little by little, letting the slowness of it intensify every sensation. I grip his shirt and lash one leg around his hip, but it's not enough. I need more contact. So I throw my arms around his neck and push my fingers into his hair while I try to climb onto his lap. The firm bulge in his trousers grows bigger and harder.

I want him inside me. I need it so badly that I feel as if I might go mad without his cock filling me up.

Derek stands up with me in his arms and sets me down on my feet. "Better stop now. I'll need at least ten minutes to cool down before we head for the house."

"No, we can't stop."

He grins. "Damn, you're cute when you want to jump my bones. But seriously, I need a cool-down period. And besides, you're, uh, having that time of the month. Right?"

Bloody hell, I forgot about that. I begged him to kiss me, and I flung my leg around him and rubbed my groin on his erection, so it's my responsibility to help him recover from a thwarted shag.

I drop to my knees in front of him.

A sweet dimple of confusion forms between his eyebrows. "Uh, what are you doing, Diana?"

"Giving you what you need." I unzip his trousers. "Can't leave you in this condition."

"I'll be fine. You don't need to—"

"Hush." I slip my hand inside his boxer shorts and slide his cock free, cradling it in my palm. "Let me do this for you."

He cups my cheek in his hand. "You really don't need to."

"You've already told me that." I grasp his cock just above the crown and glide my palm up and down his length. "I want to do it. The first time I saw you, I experienced the most intense lust I've ever known. I would've gone down on you right there in Hugh's office, but I was too dumbstruck by the sight of you to do anything."

"I wanted you at first sight too."

"Good. So shut up and let me feast on you." I slide my hand up to the base of his erection. Then I slowly rasp my tongue over the crown. "Mm, can't wait to eat you up."

Chapter Seventeen

Derek

I suck in a sharp breath as Diana drags her tongue up my dick from the crown to where her hand is still wrapped around the base. Fuck, I can't believe she's doing this. Straitlaced Diana Sangster, who only wanted me to get her pregnant, now wants to give me a blow job. That has nothing to do with our baby pact.

Diana rests one hand on my thigh as she kisses the head of my erection, then flicks the tip of her tongue on the underside. My focus is riveted to her—to what she's doing, for sure, but also to the look on her face. Her eyes drift half-closed, her lips curl up slightly at the corners, and she seems for all the world to want nothing more than to give me head.

She moves both hands onto my thighs now, gliding them up and down while she trails soft kisses along the length of my dick. Her breaths whisper out of her nostrils, teasing my skin even more. Damn, she knows what she's doing. A woman who claims she hasn't dated much shouldn't be an expert on giving head, but Diana Sangster has surprised me at every turn.

"Mm," she moans. "You taste almost as good as you feel when you're inside me."

"Uh, thanks." Can't drum up any other words. Dumb ones are all I can manage.

She grasps my dick again, holding its crown millimeters from her mouth, then puckers her lips to blow a stream of air over the head. I still have my hand in her hair, cradling her head, but that fact had flown out of my mind once she started kissing my cock. Diana flicks her tongue across the underside again, moving her tongue back and forth, side to side, while she opens her mouth and slowly takes me between her lips, drawing me into her mouth inch by inch while she lifts her gaze to me.

My dick throbs.

Diana pulls away, and the coolness of the air on my skin feels almost as erotic as her mouth. She rubs her cheek on my dick, then sucks my balls until I let out a strangled shout. While I start breathing harder, she gives my head a wet kiss with tongue, right before she slides my cock into her mouth again.

"Holy shit, Diana." I tip my head back and shut my eyes so I can just enjoy the sensations of this woman devouring my cock.

My cell phone rings.

Screw that. Whoever it is can go to hell. Diana is licking and sucking me, shoving one hand inside my pants to massage my inner thigh while her other hand crawls up my chest to pinch my nipple through my shirt. I jerk and shout. She keeps going, ravenous and determined to complete her task, and I feel an orgasm rising inside me, like an electrical current shooting down my spine and straight into my dick. I'll come soon, I know it.

My phone rings again.

I fumble to get it out of my pocket, just so I can shut the damn thing up, but then I see who's calling.

"Fuck," I snarl. "It's Avery."

Diana stops what she's doing to me, though she keeps her mouth wrapped around my erection.

I can't believe I'm doing this, but I know my sister won't give up until she gets a response from me. So, while Diana has her mouth around my dick, I answer the call. My voice comes out somewhat hoarse. "Hey, Avery, what's wrong?"

"Dinner is in eight minutes, and you're not here yet."

Uh, what is dinner? What's a minute? I have no idea.

Diana raises her brows at me.

That expression makes my dick twitch. And suddenly, I remember what those words mean. "I'll be there, don't worry. Just got, uh, distracted. See you in a few."

I punch a finger on the phone's screen to end the call.

Diana resumes licking and sucking, but she speeds up her movements. Yeah, we don't have much time. The pressure inside me has built up so hard that I know I'll come like a nuclear bomb. When she pushes her hand under my shirt and up my chest, then rakes her nails down my skin to my groin, I do exactly that. I explode inside her mouth, helpless to stop myself from thrusting.

While the last spasms fade away, my shoulders sag and my head falls forward. At my feet, Diana sits there licking her lips.

She rises and wipes dirt off her jeans. Then she smiles. "I hope you enjoyed that as much as I did."

"Hell yeah." I zip up my pants. "But we need to get back to the house before my sister sends out a search party."

"I should go first, so no one will realize we've been together."

Not sure anybody will buy that. But if it makes Diana feel better, I can roll with it. "Sure, you go first."

I move to kiss her, but she dodges it and hustles down the path. Well, I couldn't reasonably expect her to change her mind about us that fast. The fact that she not only wanted to give me head, but enjoyed doing it, makes me believe there is hope.

After a few more minutes, I tromp down the path and through the garden. It's almost dark now, but the garden has solar lights the Parrishes installed just for the wedding. Can't have guests getting lost in the dark or stumbling into the hedges. I can hear the revelry inside the house before I even reach the front steps. The door has been left open so guests can come and go as they please.

Just as I hop onto the top step, car headlights appear on the tree-shrouded stretch of the driveway that leads to the house. I thought everyone was already here, except for the Scots. They aren't supposed to arrive until tomorrow. I hop back down the steps to wait for the mysterious visitor.

Should I rush inside to alert the others? It's a bit late for that. The mystery car has just rounded the circular drive and parked at the base of the steps. The headlights shut off, and a man climbs out.

The glow from the lights inside the house casts shadows on the man's face. "Is this Sommerleigh House?"

"Yeah, it is." I walk around the car to the man standing behind its open driver's door. "Who are you? Don't think anybody else was expected tonight."

"Sorry. I got delayed and couldn't get here earlier." He offers me his hand. "I'm Dominic Rigby. Dane Dixon and I went to university together, and we've been friends ever since." His brows lift as he sweeps his gaze over me. "No offense, mate, but you don't seem like one of ours."

"If you mean I'm not a Brit, you're right." I finally accept his hand to shake it. "I'm Derek Hahn, the brother of the bride."

Dominic grins. "Oh, so you're the one Hugh mentioned. He warned me about you."

"Warned you? I'll take that as a compliment."

He shuts the car door and starts walking toward the house while I keep pace with him. "You're a bodyguard, right? Working for some insanely rich woman?"

"I own the company, so I'm a little more than a bodyguard." Though I don't like the way he described Diana, I get that he's not being offensive. I feel even more protective of her these days.

"That's brilliant. Being the man in charge must be a hard job."

"I love what I do, so I don't mind the ups and downs. What do you for a living?"

"Nothing as exciting as your line of work. I used to be a professional cricketer, but these days I coach at a private school."

I swing the door open, waving for Dominic to go inside first. "Do you mean the game cricket? I had no idea there was a professional circuit for that."

"Oh yeah, there is."

"At least now I get why Hugh insisted on setting up a cricket pitch on the lawn today." I shut the door and lead Dominic toward the dining room. "He must want you to show off your skills."

Dominic laughs. "I doubt that. Hugh has been pestering me for months about playing a game of cricket with Brits versus Scots."

"What, Americans aren't invited? How xenophobic."

"I'm sure you lot will get to participate too."

The sounds of revelry grow louder as we amble toward the dining room. Laughter erupts in between boisterous chattering and the clanking of silverware.

Just as we approach the dining room doorway, Hugh pops out and grins at us. "Finally, mate. Took you bloody long enough to get here, Dom."

"Sorry. A flat tire delayed me."

"Well, come in and join the festivities." Hugh pretends he's just now noticed me. "Oh, there you are, Derek. You're invited too, naturally."

"Gee, thanks. Your invites are always so cordial."

Hugh walks over to us and throws an arm around Dominic's shoulders. "Your girl couldn't come, eh?"

"Chelsea is not my girl. She's a mate, that's all. And she rang me earlier to say she won't be here until tomorrow."

"At least you'll have a date for the wedding." He slaps Dominic's back. "A platonic date, naturally."

Then he winks.

Dominic shakes his head and goes into the dining room.

I try to head that way, but Hugh hooks an arm around my neck to stop me. He whispers, "Did you and Diana shag in the summer house?"

"What? No." Not technically. Diana giving me head doesn't quality as sex. I think.

"Hmm. Avery wanted to hurry out to the summer house to make sure you hadn't gotten eaten by a wild animal—I kid you not—but I managed to stop her. We heard a strange noise, but I told her it must have been a fox." He leans in closer, his arm encircling my throat. "She doesn't know what foxes sound like, but I do. That was the satisfied roar of a man who just got his end away."

"Anything I might have done is none of your business." I peel his arm away. "Go lay your patented smarm on the guests, Lord Sticky."

"It's Lord Steamy. Will you never learn how to pronounce my secondary title?"

"Sure. On the day you stop butting your nose into my personal business."

He throws his hands up in surrender. "From this moment on, I shall not comment on your sexual proclivities."

"Thanks a bunch."

We walk into the dining room together, but split off to find our respective dates for the evening. Maybe Diana doesn't think she's my date, but we have been seated together at one of the two long tables that have somehow been stuffed into the space. The room is large and has always seemed kind of cavernous to me, but it feels downright cramped now, with all these wedding guests in residence.

And this group isn't even the whole crowd. The others are eating at their respective hotels, motels, and bed-and-breakfasts.

Though I take my seat beside Diana, she's talking to Dane Dixon and his wife Rika, not paying attention to me at all. Dominic has been assigned the seat next to me, so I get to talk to him some more about professional cricketing. He tells me several amazing stories about his time as an athlete. I had no idea cricket was such an exciting game. Now I'm jazzed about the matches Hugh wants to have this week. Dominic even offers to coach me so I can participate.

By the time dinner ends, I'm bushed. I stumble upstairs to my room and barely manage to undress before I collapse on the bed.

I dream about Diana's mouth wrapped around my dick.

So yeah, I need a nice long shower in the morning to get rid of the hard-on that dream gave me. Diana is the most incredible woman I've ever met, not only because of her sexual skills, but because of her intellect and determination too.

I've just walked out of the bathroom when the adjoining door is yanked open.

Diana leans against the jamb, roving her gaze over me from head to toe.

I pause in the middle of drying my hair with a towel. The rest of me is on full display, and she clearly likes getting another gander at my body.

She licks her lips. "You look good wet and clean."

"Thanks." I saunter over to her and drop the towel. "You feel good wet and dirty."

Diana is wearing her PJs, and her hair is messy, like she just crawled out of bed. I love seeing her this way. She's shown me different sides of her lately that make me want her even more—and not just for sex. I'd love to snuggle up with her in bed.

"I'll see you downstairs," she says.

Diana shuts the door.

But she hasn't shut me out. I call that a win.

Chapter Eighteen

Diana

Hugh and Avery have seen fit to seat me beside Derek during breakfast. Two days ago, I would have balked at that. But this morning, I look forward to sitting beside Derek while we enjoy a delicious meal and conversation with our friends. I haven't let a man get this close to me in years, not since my divorce, and I'm not talking about physical proximity. I shared the most painful moments of my life with Derek Hahn.

But he did the same. I've gotten to know him, and I can't deny I like what I've learned.

I also can't deny that man has a beautiful body and knows how to use all those muscles.

Despite the fact I left my room after Derek went downstairs, I still sit down at the dining room table before he does. I see Pippa at a smaller table with Rupert's daughter, and I'm glad she's enjoying herself. I'm chatting to Hugh when Derek finally ambles into the room. He smiles when he realizes the one empty chair beside mine at the table is for him. Another chair sits vacant on beside Dominic, and Hugh had mentioned that seat awaits a guest who hasn't arrived yet.

Derek settles onto his seat and leans in to whisper to me, "Are you hungry, Diana?"

"Yes, famished."

"I'd say 'ravenous' is a better description of you." He sneaks a hand onto my thigh under the table. "I see pancakes are on the menu. I'd love to take our food up to our adjoining rooms and pour syrup over your skin so I can lick—"

"Yes, I agree," I say a bit too loudly. "Pancakes are the perfect breakfast food. Let's get some of those."

Hugh smirks. Avery slants forward to peer around her brother at me, strictly so she can smile knowingly.

Dominic is seated directly across the table from me. Though I hardly know the man, he seems amused by what's happening on this side of the table. "I'd love something sweet too. Someone pass me a plate of banana pancakes, please. Those of us relegated to the healthy food section of this table demand equity in food distribution. Who wants oat bran? Give me a sugary meal."

Everyone starts chattering away and passing platters back and forth so we can all enjoy a taste of every dish. Dominic's statement also has the added benefit of distracting Avery and Hugh from noticing whatever Derek and I might say to each other.

I could kiss Dominic for that. As much as I adore the soon-to-be newlyweds, I do not like being the center of attention, particularly when that attention involves meddling.

Someone clangs a bell.

We all turn to glance at the doorway, where Kendall stands proudly holding a brass bell. "Mr. Rigby's guest has arrived. Shall I escort her into the dining room, sir?"

He looks at Hugh when he says that. At least Lord Sommerleigh has stopped wincing whenever Kendall refers to him as "sir." I think Hugh might finally be settling into his role as lord of the manor. It suits him.

"Yes, Kendall," Hugh says. "Please bring her. Dominic has been anxiously awaiting the girl's arrival."

Kendall nods crisply, turns on his heels, and strides down the hall.

Dominic aims a half-hearted scowl at Hugh. "I am not 'anxiously awaiting' anything. Focus your meddling on someone else, please." He glances conspicuously at me and Derek. "I'm not the one who needs it."

Someone chatters in the hall, the woman's voice growing louder along with her footsteps as she draws nearer to the dining room. She and Kendall halt in the doorway.

"For heaven's sake, you shouldn't make such a fuss," the American woman says. "There's no need to announce me."

Hugh twists his head around to say, "It's all right, Kendall. You can go now."

Kendall nods crisply once again and marches off down the hall.

Dominic rises from his chair. "Over here, Chelsea. We saved you a seat."

The newcomer hurries over to Dominic, who gives her a quick hug. They both sit down. The last chair has finally been occupied, which means we are at full capacity now.

"Blimey, I almost forgot to introduce you," Dominic tells the woman seated beside him. "Everyone, this is Chelsea Vance from America. We've been mates for years, and some of you have met her before. She's my guest for the wedding." He squints at Hugh when Lord Sommerleigh smirks. "But we are not a couple."

"Too bad," Reese Dixon says. "You look like you need a good shag, mate."

"Piss off, Reese."

Everyone goes back to conversing with whoever is seated nearby, and no one else harasses Dominic about his relationship with Chelsea. But I do start up a conversation with her, since she seems a bit uncomfortable in a room packed with people.

"Chelsea," I say, "I'm Diana Sangster. It's lovely to meet you."

"Thank you. It's nice to meet you too." She glances around the room, then bites down on her bottom lip. "I didn't realize how big this wedding would be. I don't recognize most of these people."

"Neither did I until they arrived for the wedding and Hugh introduced them."

"Really? I assumed I was the only one here who isn't already friends with everybody else."

"Well, I was already friends with Hugh and Avery, and her brother Derek. But the others were strangers." I sweep my gaze over the crowded room. "There are a great many people here for Lord Sommerleigh's wedding. Have you met Hugh before?"

"Yes, I have. The first time we met, he told me I could call him Lord Steamy if I wanted to. But he was joking. Hugh is quite a character."

"Wait until you meet his Scottish friends."

She laughs. "Oh yeah, Dom warned me about them."

Derek turns away from talking to his sister, apparently having overheard what Chelsea and I were discussing. He grins. "Oh-ho yeah. The MacTaggarts are a wild and crazy bunch. They'll liven up the wedding week for sure."

"I've only met a few of them," I say. "Callum is a sweet man, and I adore his wife Kate."

"But Magnus is your favorite MacTaggart. You couldn't stop staring at his tattoos." Derek turns his attention to Chelsea. "I'm Derek Hahn, by the way. The bride is my sister."

"Glad I'm not the only American here, besides the bride."

"Didn't Dominic tell you? Most of the men in this room married American women. Quite a few of the Scots married Americans too."

Chelsea glances from Derek to me and back again. "So, are you two…"

"Not dating," I say.

For the rest of breakfast, we don't discuss whether Derek and I are a couple, or whether Dominic and Chelsea are a couple. But when I had emphatically told Chelsea that I am not dating Derek, I'd felt an odd twinge of…disappointment.

After breakfast, everyone breaks up into smaller groups to go their separate ways for a while. Derek and I wind up sitting on chaises on the lawn beside Dominic and Chelsea. The cricket pitch is still set up, ready for a match. Pippa and Sally are practicing with cricket bats, but Pippa occasionally waves to me and smiles.

I've been half listening to the conversation going on at either side of me, but Chelsea says something that piques my interest.

"Did Dominic tell you what his teammates used to call him?" she asks Derek. "Back when he was a pro cricketer they gave him a nickname. He didn't like it at first, but then he decided to roll with it."

"What did they call him?" Derek asks.

"The Dom. Isn't that a great nickname? They said he dominated the pitch, so he was the Dom."

Dominic groans. "Honestly, Chelsea. That's a bloody stupid nickname. Makes me sound like I have a secret room in my basement where I tie women up."

Chelsea slants toward him. "But the Dom sounds damn sexy."

One side of his mouth kinks upward. "Well, maybe I don't hate it after all."

If these two aren't dating, they're doing a bang-on impression of a romantic couple. I suppose Derek and I have done that too. Do I want to go on pretending?

A tingle rushes over my skin, bringing with it a revelation. I no longer want to pretend that all I need from Derek is his body. Should I tell him that right now? I've always been the sort who doesn't shy away from speaking my mind, but I've done just that with Derek. After our intimate conversation yesterday, I know I need to tell him the truth about my feelings for him.

The growling of a powerful engine starts up in the distance, growing louder as the vehicle races up the driveway. By the time the motorcycle breaks out of the woods, the engine is snarling like a beast from hell. Two people sit astride the monstrosity, a man and a woman.

Derek leaps off his chaise. "Hugh! Get your ass out here! The best man has arrived."

The lawn, where we are, lies around the side of the house from the drive. I could see the motorcycle until it rounded the circular section, heading for the front of the house. Now, I can't see a thing. But I hear Hugh laughing and shouting to his best mate. Avery's voice joins Hugh's, and two less familiar voices chime in as well. That would be Callum and Kate.

Derek seizes my hand. "Come on, Diana. We should get in on the meet and greet."

He virtually drags me across the lawn, not slowing down until we've reached the front steps of Sommerleigh House. Hugh has just pulled Callum into a boisterous hug, and Kate is giving Avery a calmer version of that greeting.

Avery grins and waves when she sees us approaching.

I get dragged into a hug from the bride, while Derek joins the other men. Once the greetings are over, Hugh eyes the large black motorcycle askance.

"Did you ride that thing all the way from Scotland?" he asks. "You must have sore bums. I'm surprised you can still walk, actually."

Callum chuckles. "No, ye *cacan*, we didn't ride the Harley from Loch Fairbairn to Sommerleigh. We brought it with us on Evan's jet."

"Are you having me on? A Harley on a jet? That's ridiculous."

Kate sidles up to her husband. "Callum isn't teasing you. We really did bring the Harley onto the jet. Callum thought you guys should take a ride together before the wedding."

"Oh yes, please," Hugh says with great sarcasm. "I do love a good arse-rattling trip on the back of a snarling monster. It's so bloody relaxing."

Callum trots over to the motorcycle and retrieves a bottle from the rear compartment. He returns to us and holds the bottle out to Hugh. "Your wedding gift, from me and Kate."

"Scottish whisky?" Hugh makes a derisive noise, but it's clearly more sarcasm. "If you want to be rid of me, just run me over with your motorcycle and have done with it. No need to kill me slowly with Scottish booze."

The teasing continues, and Derek and I are invited to go into the drawing room with Hugh, Avery, Callum, and Kate. But I tell them that Derek and I need to take care of a few things. The vagueness convinces them all that we mean to do naughty things, naturally.

Derek lets me lead him into the garden, where we sit down on a concrete bench.

"What's up?" he asks. "You look like you want to tell me something."

"I do."

"Go on. I'm listening."

Suddenly, I can't think of any words to speak. This is bollocks. I've given presentations to audiences that numbered in the thousands, yet I can't tell one man how I feel. Perhaps the problem is that the only other man to whom I suggested this turned out to be a bastard. But Derek is nothing like Lyle.

Derek picks up my hand and threads his fingers with mine. "I'll go first. Diana, I care about you a lot. You're more than a client, more than a friend. You are the most incredible woman I've ever met, and I don't want to walk away from you as soon that stick turns blue."

"What stick?"

He smiles. "The pregnancy test stick."

"Oh, that." A nervous laugh bursts out of me. "I've never taken that sort of test, so I had no idea what color the sticks turns. How do you know?"

"A girl I dated once thought she was pregnant, but the home test didn't turn blue, so we knew it was a false alarm."

I study his face, while he simply gazes at me with the affection. "You would have married that girl if she had been pregnant, wouldn't you? Even if you didn't love her."

"Yes, I would have." His expression becomes pained, and though he keeps hold of my hand, he avoids my gaze. "I agreed to your terms for our deal, but I realize now that I can't do it. I can't walk away from my own child."

The time has come to tell him the truth, the one that I've denied since the moment I pushed him into that deal. "I don't want you to walk away either. In fact, I want us to have a real relationship, the romantic sort. What do you want?"

Chapter Nineteen

Derek

What do I want? Is she kidding? The truth of what I want should have been completely obvious. But I guess I've done a better job of hiding my feelings than I thought. Diana seems unaware of what I really want, which means it's my job to tell her. But I seem to have developed a sudden case of laryngitis. When I try to speak, all that comes out is a croaking sound.

Man up, you moron, and tell her.

"I want what you want, Diana." I lift her hand to my lips and kiss each knuckle. "I want you, period. And I want our baby."

"We don't have a baby yet. Not even a glimmer of one."

"Yeah, but we can change that." I slide an arm around her waist and pull her into me. Then I cradle her face in my free hand. "Think you can handle having lots of hot sex until we hit the jackpot? I'm talking about slow, steamy sex that will leave you breathless."

"I can handle that. But we'll need to wait until Saturday."

"For you, I'll wait a thousand years."

"Please don't wait that long. I need you inside me again as soon as possible."

I brush a kiss over her lips. "Would midnight on Saturday work for you?"

She laughs softly. "Yes, darling, that works for me."

"You just called me 'darling.' Never heard you say that to anyone before."

"I've never wanted to refer to any man that way, not even Lyle. And I call Pippa 'dear' or 'pet.' "

Diana has a special word for me. I like that. No, I *love* that. But I can't think of a pet name for her. So instead, I draw her closer and kiss her.

"There they are!" Pippa shouts.

I glance over my shoulder. Pippa, Avery, and Hugh have just entered the garden, and now, thanks to the teenager's exclamation, all three of them see me and Diana on the bench. They probably saw us kissing too.

Pippa races up to us and grins. "You are dating, aren't you?"

I look at Diana, but she just shrugs. "We weren't dating ten minutes ago, but we are now."

"That's right," Diana says.

Pippa claps her hands, jumping up and down while she shrieks. "I knew it! I knew it! You'll be getting married next."

Avery and Hugh have come up beside Pippa. My sister seems way too pleased with herself, like she always knew Diana and I would get together. Well, I guess Avery kind of did figure that out a while ago. That's damn annoying, and I will never concede the point. It's a big brother's prerogative.

Especially when his sister has been meddling. Adjoining bedrooms? Yeah, that trick alone gives me an excuse not to acknowledge she was right.

Pippa and the happy couple keep grinning at us.

"Did you guys have a reason to hunt us down?" I ask. "Or are you lost on your own estate, Lord Sticky?"

Hugh tries to stop grinning, but his lips keep twitching up at the corners. "We would like to play cricket, but Dominic wants to give you a crash course on the rules of the game before we do that."

"I don't need to participate. All you weirdos can play with your balls while I hang out with the ladies."

"Have you ever played baseball or American football?"

"Yeah, sure. I've done both."

"Then you'll enjoy cricket. It's reminiscent of both baseball and football, but it's far more exciting than either. Why not give it a go?" He bends over to stare straight into my eyes. "Unless you're afraid the Brits will beat you."

I snort. "Please. You pansies don't have a chance."

Hugh's lips curve into a sneaky smile. "I think we'll put you on the Scots' team. They are large, arrogant, and vicious."

"Your best friend is a Scot."

"And that's how I know what they're like."

I sigh and stand up. "I know those plaid fanatics. They love me. But only one Scot is here, so it's a rigged game."

Hugh's sneaky smile returns. "The rest of them arrived while you and Diana were snogging." He pulls a walkie-talkie out of his back pocket and holds it near his face. "Chance, are you there?"

"Yes," comes the response. That's Chance Dixon, one of Hugh's buddies. "Did you find the missing couple?"

"We did. So tell the Scots they can start the celebration."

"Understood."

Hugh shoves the walkie-talkie back into his pocket, still seeming way too pleased with himself.

Then I find out why. Bagpipe music erupts from the direction of the lawn. First, it's just low droning. But soon, the familiar sound of the pipes blares, playing a traditional Scottish tune—"Scotland the Brave."

If Hugh expected me to bitch about the music, he doesn't know me as well as he thinks. I clap my hands and holler, "Oh, yeah! Now that's more like it. Let's go out there and get dancing."

Hugh gapes at me. "You like Scottish music?"

"Sure do. I hung out with the MacTaggarts during Kate and Callum's wedding bash. They even taught me a few dance steps."

"I had no idea you liked dancing."

"Don't look so shocked. Brits aren't the only ones who have charm and sophistication." I slap his arm. "Relax, buddy. I won't steal your prized title. You'll always be Lord Sticky to me."

He shakes his head and sighs. Then he leads our little procession out of the garden toward the lawn, which now holds more than a cricket pitch. A horde of wedding guests has gathered there too, and the bagpipe music has stopped.

Dominic jogs over to us just as we reach the corner of the house. "Derek, it's time for your crash course. Hugh, join the rest of our team. It's Brits versus Scots with a few Americans to fill out the teams. Since we don't have enough for eleven players on each side, we've settled for ten instead. There will also be only one umpire."

"How could we have ten players?" Hugh asks. "The Scots have that many, but I'm fairly certain we Brits only have eight men. Nine if Alex Thorne breaks away from the Scots. But that would mean convincing Catriona that her husband is not betraying her clan."

"Alex is British. Catriona forgives him for defecting to our side."

"Doesn't Alex have American citizenship too?" I ask.

"Yes," Dominic says. "But he chooses to play for the Brits in this game. Luke Turner is one hundred percent American, though his wife is Scottish, but he's defecting to our team with Kirsty's approval."

"All the married men do whatever their wives tell them, hey? The ladies really have them by the short hairs."

Diana rises onto her tiptoes to whisper to me, "Won't you do whatever I say and let me take you by the short hairs?"

The sexy tone of her voice makes me cough into my fist.

Dominic and Hugh both smirk.

To change the subject, I ask, "Any other Americans on the teams?"

"Yes," Dominic says. "You will fill out the Scots team as their sole American player."

"Me and nine Scots. Awesome. We'll whup you guys so bad you'll need your wives to finish the game for you."

Dominic shakes his head. "I'm not married. Neither is Errol Murdoch, a closet MacTaggart, though he is engaged to a beautiful American."

"What the heck is a closet MacTaggart?"

"Errol's mother was born a MacTaggart, but his father belonged to the Murdoch clan."

"Uh-huh." Don't think I'll try to study Scottish genealogy. It sounds way too complicated. "Okay, I'm ready for that crash course."

I kiss Diana goodbye, then follow Dominic to the far side of the lawn and around the back of the house. Apparently, he thinks I need to be shielded from view in case I tank this crash course. Cricket can't be that hard. I played football in high school and got tackled once in a while. I doubt this British game is harder than football.

But Dominic reminds me that we're in England now, where football is a different game, what Americans call soccer. I play it cool and don't point out that British football is nowhere near as rough as the American version. Don't want to annoy my coach before the big cricket match.

First, Dominic needs to explain the terminology of the game. "When you're the batsman, your job is to stop the bowler from hitting the wicket."

"Huh? Not sure you're speaking English. As much as I'd love to think I'm Batman, I don't get what a comic book character has to do with cricket."

"Not Batman. The batsman. Listen to how I'm pronouncing it. Bats-min. Not bat-man."

I might take offense at his over-enunciation, but I can tell he's not being snarky. Dominic genuinely wants to get me up to speed with a game I've never seen before, much less played. So, as our tutorial continues, I listen and ask questions only when necessary. Cricket doesn't seem that difficult. I don't need to be an expert, though, since this is a casual match strictly for fun.

The bat is a long, flat piece of wood with a handle. Okay, at least that somewhat resembles a baseball bat, so I can handle that. But when Dominic starts talking about wickets and bails, I know this game is not as much like baseball as I'd hoped.

Shinty would've been a better option for me. I've played that Scottish sport. British sports…not so much. But this is just a game for fun. Doesn't matter if I suck at it.

Once our crash course has ended, I tell Dominic, "You're a great coach. Thanks for all the pointers."

"Glad to help."

"Where do you coach, by the way? Just curious. You mentioned a private school."

He winces a little and shoves his hands into his pants pockets. "I coach at a girls' school."

"Nothing wrong with that."

"It's not the most, ah, masculine job for a man who's known as the Dom."

"Don't you like your job anymore?"

He hunches his shoulders. "I love it."

"That's great. You shouldn't feel embarrassed about teaching girls. I mean, Dane Dixon used to design sex toys for women, and Hugh makes candy."

"Good point." A slow smile stretches his lips. "I should harass Hugh about being a candy maker, shouldn't I?"

"Absolutely."

We head back out onto the big lawn, where the pitch waits for us and our teammates. The wickets have been set up, and I now know those are three stakes, called stumps, that have two crosspieces or bails set on top of them. A wicket stands at each end of the playing area. Our umpire is Evan MacTaggart, a Scot, but everybody agrees he will be fair. Plus, he's played cricket before and knows the rules.

Not sure if the other Scots are well-versed in the ins and outs of cricket. Since they play shinty like it's a death match and rules are something to scoff at, I have a feeling they'll treat cricket the same way.

Before we take the field, every player is given one piece of safety equipment—legguards, which are pads that protect the shins and knees. When Evan asks if players should have gloves and helmets too, the Brits laugh.

Question answered, I guess.

Hugh requests a last-minute change to the player lineup. Callum wants to play on his best friend's team, so he switches to the British side while Luke comes over to the Scottish team.

Now we're ready to play.

As we jog out onto the field, the ladies rush over to kiss their husbands and fiances. Some of the women get, uh, very affectionate about how they provide moral support to their guys. But when Avery kisses Hugh, I have to turn my head away. No, I do not need to watch my baby sister making out with Lord Sticky, especially since I saw her grabbing his ass right before she did things I refused to watch.

After the other ladies have finished their good luck spectacle, Diana walks up to me.

"You can just tell me good luck," I say. "You don't need to feel obligated to—"

She grasps my face with both hands, raises onto her tiptoes, and mashes her lips to mine. With her entire body plastered to mine, I lose the ability to think rationally. That means I wrap my arms around Diana and tug her into me while we ravage each other's mouths like the world is about to explode.

Cheers and cat calls erupt around us.

Diana peels her lips away, but then gives me a quick kiss. "Kick their arses, darling."

"You want me to whup your fellow Brits?"

"Of course. I root for my man."

Diana spins around and sashays over to the line of chairs where the other ladies have taken their seats. She drops onto the chaise beside Avery.

Oh yeah, my team is going to wallop the Brits for sure. Diana just gave me all the inspiration I need to get the job done.

I face the two teams and shout, "What are you waiting for? Let's kick the shit out of each other."

The guys all raise their bats and cheer.

Chapter Twenty

Diana

The man I adore is about to engage in a sport he has never played before, with teammates who have a bizarre idea about what sports are meant to be like. I talked to some of the MacTaggart wives while Derek was off getting a crash course in cricket. Those women told me how the MacTaggarts often ignore the rules and will do almost anything to win a match, whether it's shinty, football, or cricket. The Scottish team will win, they say.

But the British wives told me their men are experts at cricket, and they will certainly win.

At least the players all have legguards.

That might not help with this lot. After spending several hours with them, I've decided they seem likely to ignore the rules just for fun.

I can't hear it, but I can see the teams having brief discussions that I assume are about strategy. Then two men from each team take up positions at the wickets. The rest spread out around the field.

"What's going on?" Avery asks.

"Evan MacTaggart has taken his position as umpire. Hugh is the first batsman, and Magnus MacTaggart is the bowler. That means Magnus will pitch the ball and Hugh will hit it with his bat. Errol Murdoch is positioned behind Hugh so he can catch the ball if Hugh misses it. And Chance Dixon is standing near Magnus so he can make a run."

"This is more like baseball than I expected. Well, except for those wicket thingies."

"Shh, it's time for the first bowl."

Avery leans forward in her chaise, hands clasped under her chin.

Hugh runs toward his wicket and hurls the ball at the other end of the pitch. It smacks into the bail, knocking it off the stumps.

"Does that mean he won?" Avery asks.

"No, dear, it means he bowled out. It's like a strike in baseball."

"Oh no, poor Hugh."

My gaze wanders around the field until I finally spot Derek. He's waiting for a chance to catch a ball, like most of the men on the lawn. Maybe I should root for the British team, but I want Derek to beat them.

Avery is chewing on her lower lip.

"Don't worry," I tell her. "Hugh is no bunny. He'll do better next time."

"Bunny? I know he's not a rabbit."

"No, dear, bunny is a cricket term. It means someone who is easy to dismiss."

"Oh. Well, Hugh definitely isn't that." She flashes me a knowing smile. "Neither is Derek."

No one would ever apply that term to Derek Hahn. He is the quintessential tough guy, like Sylvester Stallone without his arsenal of weapons. Now that I no longer need to pretend that I don't want Derek, as a lover and a boyfriend, I'm free to scream my bloody head off when he makes the winning hit in this match.

But I still feel odd referring to him as my boyfriend. I'm forty-five years old, not a teenager. Am I too old for him? He is a virile man in his thirties. If I can't get pregnant soon, I will never be able to give him a child of his own.

"Look!" Avery says. "Hugh just hit the ball, and it flew past Magnus. Then Richard Hunter caught it. Woo-hoo! Go, Rick! Go, Lord Steamy!"

She actually calls Hugh that? In public?

I should invent a nickname for Derek. Something sexier than Hugh's moniker. I'll need to think about that.

"Are you sure that wasn't Nick Hunter who caught the ball?" I ask. "They are twins, after all."

"Oh, that was definitely Rick. Maddie jumped up and down when he made that catch, and I think his wife can tell the brothers apart."

"I'm sure you're right. I can't tell them apart, but apparently you can."

Avery gives my hand a squeeze. "You just met them yesterday. It'll take time to for you to sort out the twins."

I sit forward and crane my neck to see the players on the pitch. "When will Derek have his turn as batsman?"

Avery touches my hand. "I'm so glad you guys finally admitted you're a couple. That means we'll be sisters, eventually."

"Let's not get ahead of ourselves, pet. Derek and I have only just become a couple."

"But you've known each other longer than Hugh and I had when we said the L-word. I fell for him the day after we met, but I resisted those feelings at first." She squeezes my hand again. "You guys have known each other for three months."

"Well, technically, yes." I resist the impulse to squirm in my chaise. I've handled recalcitrant clients without experiencing a trace of anxiety. Yet Avery's discussion of whatever feelings she believes Derek and I should be experiencing gives me an itchy sensation under my skin.

Two women approach us, halting near our chaises. The one who has toffee-brown hair slants toward me to hold out her hand. "We haven't been properly introduced. I'm Serena MacTaggart, Logan's wife. He's the stepdad of my son, Chase. Pippa has been hanging out with him and Malina. She's the daughter of Iain and Rae MacTaggart."

A stranger has just thrown a cornucopia of names at me. I had noticed an older teenager talking to Pippa. When I glance around, I see another teenage girl has joined them.

The other woman, who has dark hair, comes up beside Serena to offer me her hand while cradling a toddler in her arms. "I'm Keely MacTaggart, Evan's wife. This is our daughter, Joy. Serena and I wanted to welcome you to the fold."

"What fold?" I ask. "I'm not the wife of a Scotsman."

"No, but you are like us—women who fell for men from other countries. We'd like to give you preemptive membership in the American Wives Club, British Branch, and our subcommittee, the Mature Wives Club."

"I've heard of the American Wives Club, thanks to Hugh and Avery. But no one mentioned a subcommittee. Are you lot forming your own country?"

Keely grins. "Wouldn't it be amazing if we did? But no, we're just a group of like-minded people who want to help our friends and loved ones. Everyone we have helped thanked us in the end."

I can't help watching these women with a skeptical eye. "How precisely do you 'help' them?"

"We meddle," Serena says. "With love and our own kind of tact."

"I see. And what does your subcommittee do?"

"We just formed that subcommittee, so we'll need time to figure out how we can better serve the Club. But this new group consists of mature men and women. That means people over forty, like me and Keely. Oh, and Iain too."

"What about the Hunter boys? Aren't they in that age bracket as well?"

"Yes, they are. We haven't created an official roster yet."

I settle back in my chair. "I can't join your club. I am not anyone's wife."

Avery wags her eyebrows. "Not yet."

Good lord, these women are determined. I would admire that under any other circumstances, but not now. I arch my brows at Avery. "When we met, you were a serious-minded professional who would never have joined such a barmy group."

"I still am a professional, and I take image consulting very seriously. But this is my wedding week. It's a time to cut loose, party hearty, and throw caution to the wind."

What about me makes her believe I will ever do those things? Perhaps I should do. If I can remember how to "throw caution to the wind." Have I ever done that before? It's doubtful.

A figure flies by, just missing Keely and Serena. They jump sideways, revealing the man who lies prone on the ground. Callum leaps up and brushes dirt and grass off his clothes.

"Pardon me, lasses," he says. "I was trying to catch that ball before Lachlan could grab it, and I got a wee bit too enthusiastic about winning."

His shirt is soaked with sweat. He glances down at himself, shrugs, then whips his shirt off and tosses it to his wife. Kate sits on a regular lawn chair rather than a chaise, but at least eight other chairs lie between us and Kate. Still, Callum sent his shirt flying past all those other chaises and chairs, where it landed on Kate's calves.

Now that's talent.

Kate hugs the shirt to her chest and blows a kiss to her husband.

Callum grins and gives the thumbs-up sign to our little group. "Best watch the game, lasses. It's about to get very exciting."

"You don't mind playing for the other side?" I say. "Your own brother is playing against you."

"Hugh is my best mate, and this is his wedding week. I'll trounce every MacTaggart, even Magnus, to give Hugh the win."

Callum jogs back out onto the field.

Not only does he have impressive physical prowess, but Callum also has a quality that's too rare these days—loyalty.

Avery jerks upright, straddling her chaise, her eyes alight with excitement. "Look, it's Derek's turn. He's the batsman."

"We'll leave you guys to watch the game," Serena says. "We're maritally obligated to root for the Scots."

The two ladies walk away.

Avery clasps her hands, tucking them under her chin.

Derek stands behind the wicket, tapping his bat on the ground. Hugh steps up to the other wicket, clearly meaning to take his position as bowler.

"Oh, no," Avery says. "Who do I root for now? Derek is my brother, but Hugh is my fiance. What jerk pitted them against each other? Whoever it was, I'll give them a piece of my mind."

"I have a solution. Let me root for Derek, so you can cheer Hugh on. Derek will forgive you."

"No, I can't do that. I'll have to cheer for both of them, no sides."

Pippa races up from behind me and bends over between our chaises. She brings out a sheet of paper, offering it to Avery. "Derek asked me to give this to you."

She unfolds the paper—and smiles. "Derek says I have to cheer for Hugh, and if he catches me not rooting for Lord Sticky, he'll disown me." She shakes her head, still smiling. "He's joking. But I know he honestly wants me to cheer for Hugh."

"Yes, Derek is right about that. He's a very intelligent man."

We both turn our attention to the lawn. Derek stands ready to hit the ball, waiting for Hugh to bowl. The men stare at each other without expression. Aidan MacTaggart has taken up a position at Hugh's end of the pitch, prepared to race over to the other side the moment Hugh throws that ball.

Everyone on the lawn has fallen silent. All eyes converge on the pitch as we all wait for *that* moment.

I watch Derek. My fingers dig into my thighs, and I swear my heart is beating faster.

Hugh throws the ball. It flies through the air toward Derek, who swings his bat just in time. The crack of the strike echoes off the house, and Aidan bolts for the other end of the pitch. Meanwhile, the ball sails through the air, and every man on the field wants to be the one to catch it.

Nick Hunter from the British team leaps out, reaching for the ball. But Iain MacTaggart snatches it away before Nick can even touch it.

Cheers erupt. Even the wives of the Brits whoop and clap for the Scots team.

The game goes on, and Derek hits another ball that one of his teammates catches. Every man, woman, and child on the lawn cheers, no matter which side caught the ball. This match it strictly for fun, after all.

Once the match ends, Errol Murdoch raises his arms high and shouts, "We have all agreed, the Scots won! You know what that means." He grins. "It's taps off, laddies!"

Both teams whip their shirts off and fling them away.

Then they sprint over to the spectators to find their respective loved ones. Avery leaps off her chaise and throws herself at Hugh. He lashes his arms around her, lifting his fiancee off the ground as they kiss passionately.

I stand up and wait for Derek to rush over to me, though I doubt he will show as much passion as Hugh and Avery did.

Derek halts a few feet from me, breathing hard, sweat glistening on his bare chest. His joyful smile makes my heart skip a beat.

Then I fling myself at him. Not a bloody clue why I do that. The impulse struck, and I couldn't resist it. Derek hugs me tightly to his body and kisses me. While he slips his tongue between my lips, I melt into him, and the rest of the world fades away. He kisses me like we haven't seen each other in years, and he's spent all that time lost on a desert island.

Cat calls and whistles erupt around us.

When Derek finally sets me down on my feet, I'm breathless. My cheeks feel warm too, and so do the most intimate parts of my body. He brushes the backs of his fingers over my cheek.

And I don't even care that everyone is watching us.

Chapter Twenty-One

Derek

Even a few days after it happened, I can't believe Diana kissed me in front of everyone. And that was no peck on the lips. She went all in with that kiss, holding nothing back. That makes me wonder if she's ready to do the same with our relationship, but I haven't gotten the chance to talk to her about that. I'd been waylaid and talked into helping out with the preparations for the big wedding, from the groom's side of things, and Diana got roped into assisting the ladies with prep for the decorations and making sure the bride has everything she needs.

My sister is getting married today. In a matter of hours, Avery will become Lady Sommerleigh. *Holy shit.*

I've finished all my tasks for today, and Hugh is as ready as he'll ever be to tie the knot. Avery had asked me yesterday if I could "please, please, please" take a break from harassing Hugh until after the ceremony. I agreed, of course. I seriously doubt he gives a damn if I harass him, since that's just the way we communicate with each other, but I'll do anything for my sister.

She didn't ask me not to razz Hugh at the reception…

I glance at my watch and realize it's time for me to get dressed for the ceremony. Hugh had suggested a more laid-back style for himself and his groomsmen, but Avery begged him to do something special, and the guy just can't say no to her. So when I jog upstairs to change clothes, I put on a formal suit with tails and fancy collars. My shoes are so shiny that they almost blind me every time I look down.

Someone knocks on the bedroom door just as I'm checking myself in the mirror to make sure I got everything right.

"Come in," I holler.

A click tells me my visitor has entered the room.

I turn around—and my jaw drops. I swear it does. Diana sashays up to me wearing a gray dress that clings to her figure. Spaghetti straps hold up the modest neckline, and gray high heels boost her height just enough that we're almost eye to eye when she halts in front of me. Her hair has been styled in loose curls that kiss her cheeks.

She spins around once. "How do you like this? I wanted to wear something plainer, but the bride insisted I had to choose a formal dress. She helped me shop for one."

For a moment, all I can do is shake my head slowly. "Damn, you look incredible."

"So do you."

Pippa appears in the doorway, wearing a flower-print dress. She has her hair spiffed up too.

"I'm one lucky guy," I say. "After the ceremony, I get to escort the two most beautiful girls in the world to the reception. I hope you'll save a dance for me, Pippa."

The kid hunches her shoulders and smiles shyly.

I take that as a yes.

"Avery sent me," Pippa says. "It's time to go downstairs. The wedding will start soon."

"You go ahead," Diana says. "We'll be there shortly."

Pippa skips out of sight.

Diana fingers my tie. "You look so good in this suit that I want to slam that door and beg you to take me right now."

"Yeah, I feel the same way about your dress."

She slants in to whisper in my ear, "This is Saturday. That means after the reception, we can get back to work on making a baby. We did make an appointment for midnight."

With all the wedding craziness, I'd almost forgotten about that. Since we're now dating, I need to ask her something. "Is this still about our deal?"

"No."

"Are you still planning to send me away to America?"

She shakes her head, and her hair tickles my cheek. "I want to have a baby with you, Derek. I want us to raise our child together. Can you handle that?"

"Yes, ma'am, Ms. Sangster."

Diana grasps my tie and uses it like a leash to lead me out of the bedroom. She only releases it when we reach the stairs. Then she flashes me a sexy smile as we walk down the steps hand in hand.

Tonight, I will make love to Diana. Not because of that cockamamie deal. Not because I'm her donor. We will make love for real this time, and I know we'll make a baby. I can feel it. Don't care if that makes no sense.

Just as we get to the front door, which hangs open, I grasp Diana's elbow to stop her. She turns to look at me, a question in her eyes. I clasp her face in my hands and just say it.

"I love you, Diana."

Her lips gradually curl into a sweet smile. "I love you too, Derek."

Then I kiss her. It's a simple, sweet meeting of our lips, but it conveys everything we both feel for each other. I've never been the mushy type, but right now, I want to act the way Avery and Hugh have been behaving because I finally get why they've been that way. Love makes a man stupid in the best way.

Just as we're about to leave the house, Kate MacTaggart sprints up to us, breathing hard. "Avery wants to see you, Derek."

"What's wrong?"

"Nothing. She just wants to talk to you before the ceremony."

Kate is the matron of honor, since Avery didn't have close friends until after she met Hugh. He introduced her to the Dixons, Hunters, and the Scots. Callum is married to Kate, and he's Hugh's best friend, so the two women have become close too. It made sense for Kate to stand beside Avery during the wedding.

"Where is Avery?" I ask.

"In the drawing room."

"Okay, I'll be there in a minute." As Kate hurries away, I look at Diana. "Guess I won't see you again until after the ceremony."

"Pippa and I will be in the front row."

I give her a quick kiss. "See you soon."

Then I jog down the hall to the drawing room. The door hangs partway open, and I can see Kate standing just inside, talking to someone. I assume it's Avery, but I can't see her. When Kate spots me, she smiles and comes out into the hallway.

"See you at the altar," she says.

Then Kate hurries away.

I step into the drawing and freeze. My throat goes thick. I force my feet to carry me closer, but the sight of my sister all gussied up for her wedding suddenly affects me so strongly that I can't speak, not even when I halt an arm's length away.

Her wedding dress is covered in lace, with shiny little beads sewn onto it, and the flowing skirt swishes with her slightest movement. The veil features the same lace and beads, but it doesn't cover her face. It hangs off the back of her head to show off her hair and its zillions of little curls that must have taken hours to create.

The engagement ring on her finger sparkles in the sunlight that pours through the windows.

"Avery, I—" My throat tightens up, and I can't finish whatever I'd been about to say.

She holds out her hands to me.

I clasp them and let her draw me closer. Then I finally manage to speak a full sentence. "Kate said you wanted to talk to me."

She nods, her eyes glistening. "We've been through a lot, haven't we? Losing Mom and Dad. Me working too damn hard, and you always watching out for me. I wasn't at all surprised when you became a bodyguard. You are a protector, Derek. But you don't need to protect me anymore."

"I know that. You're a strong, compassionate, amazing woman, Avery." I nod toward the ceiling. "Mom and Dad are up there watching us, and I know they're as proud of the woman you've become as I am."

She sucks in a ragged breath, and her eyes are glistening even more.

"Don't cry," I say. "It'll ruin your makeup, and Kate will murder me for that."

"It's waterproof makeup." She grips my hands more firmly. "We've never been the kind of family who gush all the time, but I need to tell you this now. I love you, Derek, love you so much."

Tears pool in my eyes, and though I try to swipe them away, new ones form in their place. "I love you too, Avery. You found your soul mate, and I'm looking forward to playing with all those little half-British babies you're going to have."

She laughs even while crying and throws her arms around me. For a moment, we just hold on to each other and let the tears flow. Then we pull away and dry our eyes. Avery's makeup really is waterproof, so she doesn't have any streaks on her face. Her eyes are a little red, but that will go away by the time she reaches the altar.

I kiss her cheek and escort her into the foyer, where the matron of honor and the other bridesmaids wait for her. I trot out of the house, but I don't make a beeline for the altar. I'll take my place beside Callum later. First, I need to walk the bride down the aisle. That means I stop just outside the door and wait for Avery.

The rest of the groom's party has already joined Hugh at the altar. His cousin Rupert fills out the groom's side, while the bride's side will include Kate and two others—Maddie and Rika, the wives of Richard Hunter and Dane Dixon. In the crowd, I see rows and rows of Brits and Scots and Americans who have known Avery for three months but treat her like a member of their collective family. They've treated me that way too, and their generosity never ceases to amaze me.

The music starts up, and everyone turns to watch the bridesmaids march up the aisle. I step aside to make room for them, then move into position. Once those ladies have reached their posts, the music shifts to the bridal march.

My sister steps up beside me and hooks her arm around mine. Then we stroll up the aisle together. I get a pang in my chest, but it's not painful or unpleasant. Never thought I'd see the day my workaholic sister settled down and really started to live her life. But here she is, walking up to the altar to pledge her heart to the love of her life.

As we reach the altar, I kiss her cheek and whisper, "You found a good one, and Hugh's one lucky bastard."

I wink, then take my position beside Callum.

Somehow I keep my cool while she steps up beside Hugh, and while the minister does his thing and the bride and groom exchange their vows. But when Hugh kisses Avery, and the crowd erupts in cheers, the emotions of this day finally hit me—and I get choked up.

The minister announces, "It is my great pleasure to introduce Lord and Lady Sommerleigh."

Avery tosses the bouquet.

Diana catches it. But I don't think she meant to do that. It seemed like a reflex, and she looked stunned when she realized she was holding the flowers.

Would I want to marry Diana? It's too soon for that, but I already know the answer. Yes, I would marry her. No woman on earth has ever made me feel as good as Diana Sangster does. Avery suggested Diana might be my soul mate, but I'd brushed that off as romantic nonsense. Now, as I watch Hugh and Avery hurrying back down the aisle while grinning and laughing, I realize I want that nonsense to be true.

Once the newlyweds have gone into the house, I weave through the crowd to find Diana and Pippa. We're part of the group that will see the newlyweds off, as they head to a super swanky hotel in London for their wedding night. Then they'll be off to a private island in the Caribbean, where a famous and reclusive author lives. Richard Hunter has become friends with Sir Dexter Armstrong-Hill, so he had no trouble convincing the man to let Hugh and Avery honeymoon on his island. He loves guests, as long as Richard has vouched for them.

But Hugh and Avery won't take off until they've spent some time at the reception. That event takes place in the garden and spills out onto the front lawn.

I dance with every woman in attendance, I think. But my sister gets first dibs, after she and Hugh enjoy their first dance as a married couple. Once we're on the floor, spinning slowly, I smirk and ask her, "So, is that moratorium on harassing Hugh still in effect? You said don't do that before or during the wedding, but this is the reception."

She throws her head back and laughs.

Chapter Twenty-Two

Diana

I've danced with so many men tonight that I have trouble remembering the names of most of them. I'd met these gents over the past few days. That didn't allow much time for memorizing names and the faces attached to them. I've enjoyed every moment, particularly when I danced with Rupert and Callum, but I still haven't gotten the chance to take a spin with Derek. Not that I blame the other women in attendance for monopolizing his time. Derek Hahn is attractive, sexy, and personable.

Every woman who spends a few minutes in his arms winds up laughing so loudly that I can hear it from the other side of the dance floor. This is an outdoor event, so the "floor" consists of tiles raised slightly above the grass beneath them.

My partner at the moment is Bennett Montague, a member of the Mithorian royal family. I can't deny I'm intrigued by what I've heard about him, and since I am never shy about asking questions, I "grill" him, as Derek would say.

"Are you still a royal?" I ask. "Someone mentioned that you abdicated your role as crown prince."

"I'm still royal. But yes, I gave up the crown. My sister Stephanie loves all that royal rubbish, so now she is the crown princess." He executes an impressive series of steps to keep us from tripping off the edge of the dance floor. "My family understood why I needed to go my own way, and they've been very supportive. So have my mates."

"You must've had a long flight to get here from Mithoria. It's in the middle of the Atlantic Ocean, isn't it?"

"That's right. But Sam and I don't live there. I think you met my wife Samantha earlier. We visit Mithoria several times a year, but our home is in Cockshire."

My brows lift. "I've never heard of Cockshire."

"It's a little village in Essex. That's where Nick and Siobhan Hunter live too. I work for Nick at his day spa, Nick's Nirvana."

"You are a massage therapist?"

"I am, and I love my job. Sam is a virtual assistant, so she can work from anywhere."

A hand appears on Bennett's shoulder. "May I cut in, mate?"

Ben swivels his head to see Hugh. "She's all yours, Lord Sommerleigh."

The former crown prince walks away, and Hugh clasps my hand as we begin to glide across the floor. He is a superb dancer, very light on his feet and always aware of his partner's needs. I imagine he's like that with Avery too, even when they aren't dancing.

"I wanted to talk to you," he says, "and this seemed like the best way to get you alone."

"We're surrounded by enough people to form our own village."

"You know what I meant." He deftly avoids Reese and Arden Dixon, since the couple seems too focused on each other to notice us. "I need to thank you, Diana. Avery saved my soul, but you saved my company and my family's legacy. I will always be grateful to you for that, more grateful than words can express."

"I provided capital and advice, that's all. You did the rest."

He smiles and sighs. "I had a feeling you wouldn't accept the credit."

"Of course I wouldn't. I work in the background. Taking the credit is not how I do things."

"That won't stop me from being grateful." He glances at something past my shoulder, then he halts us and kisses my hand. "Thank you for a lovely dance, Diana."

Hugh disappears into the crowd, and Derek takes his place.

"May I have this dance?" he asks. "I'm not as smooth as Hugh, but I won't step on your feet."

"I've seen you dancing with other women." As he clasps my hand and we begin to move, I experience a sudden flutter in my belly. "You are an excellent dancer. With your looks and charm, you could have any woman you want."

He pulls me snugly against his body. "I've got the woman I want."

That flutter intensifies, and warmth rushes through me. "Do we still have a date for midnight?"

"Can we move that up? Don't think I can wait until midnight." He twirls us around, then dips his head to whisper in my ear, "Let's go upstairs as soon as we see the newlyweds off."

"Oh, thank goodness. I was afraid you'd insist on waiting until midnight."

"No way." His voice becomes deeper and more sensual as he murmurs, "I've never seen you naked, except from the waist down."

"That changes tonight."

Derek's mobile chimes. He pulls the device out to check what must be a text message, then tucks the mobile back into his pocket. "It's time for the send-off."

While the revelry continues all around us, we briskly walk around the house to the driveway, hand in hand. Rupert, Pippa, Sally, Callum, and Kate have joined Hugh and Avery at the bottom of the steps. A limousine waits for the newlyweds. But first, we need to say goodbye.

The limousine will take them to London for a night at the most expensive hotel in the city. Then tomorrow, they'll fly to Elusion Island for their Caribbean honeymoon on Dexter Armstrong-Hill's private getaway. These two deserve the best of everything.

Rupert hugs his cousin and jokes with him, then Pippa gives Hugh and Avery big hugs while grinning. Rupert's wife had taken their son upstairs to put him to bed for the night, but their daughter Sally stayed with her father. Now, she gives Hugh and Avery big hugs too. Kate goes next, offering her goodbyes and good wishes. Then Callum steps up to his best friend.

He hauls Hugh into a bear hug, thumping him on the back. Then he steps back and slaps Hugh's arm. "Shag a lot and drink plenty of champagne. You're one lucky sod to convince a woman like Avery to marry a *cacan* like you."

Callum grins and winks at the bride.

Hugh pulls his wife close and gazes at her with genuine love. "Yes, I am one lucky sod."

Callum moves aside.

I hug Hugh and kiss his cheek. But when I do the same for Avery, she whispers to me, "Can't wait for you to become my sister-in-law."

There's no point in telling her yet again that it's too early to discuss that possibility. I know she means well, and I do adore Avery.

Derek faces Hugh, and the two men smirk at each other for a moment. Then Derek says, "Don't let my sister get sunburned, Lord Sticky."

"I shall guard her skin as if it were my own."

Derek gives Hugh a quick, firm hug. Then he turns to his sister, and his attitude shifts from sarcasm to affection, his love for his sister evident on his face—and in his voice when he speaks. "All I've ever wanted was for you to be happy, really happy. I'm glad you finally stopped working so hard and found everything you needed."

Avery throw her arms around her brother, and tears trickle down her cheeks.

When she finally steps back, Derek wipes the tears away with his thumb. "These are happy tears, right?"

She nods.

"Good." He glances at Hugh, pretending to glare at Lord Sommerleigh. "Because if that guy hurts my sister, I'll rip him a new one."

Avery slaps his arm. "Stop harassing Hugh."

"Why? He likes it. Don't you, Lord Sticky?"

"Oh, yes," Hugh says. "I love your bizarre American insults."

Now that the goodbyes are over, Hugh opens the limo door and offers Avery his hand to climb inside. Once the door shuts, we can't see them anymore. The vehicle rolls down the drive and out of sight.

Rupert goes inside the house to find his wife, with his daughter in tow, while Callum and Kate head back to the party on the lawn.

"It's time for bed, pet," I tell Pippa.

She starts up the steps but halts halfway to the top. "Good night, Derek. Good night, Diana."

Hearing her use my given name, I abruptly realize I need to do something I've avoided for too long. "I'd like it if you would call me Mum."

Her eyes widen. "Really? You never wanted that."

"A lot has changed. I can't believe I wouldn't let you call me that."

"So I can now?" When I nod, she rushes down the steps to hug me. Then she looks at me. "Good night, Mum."

Pippa scampers into the house.

But Derek just stands there on the pea gravel, gazing down the tree-shrouded drive though he can't see anything in the darkness.

I slip my arm around his waist. "You miss her already, don't you?"

"Yeah. It's stupid, since she'll only be gone for two weeks. And she was jetting around the world for years, so it's not like I saw her all the time then."

"But since she met Hugh, Avery has settled down. You see much more of her now, and you two have become even closer."

He hooks his arm around me. "Things will be different now that she's married."

"Of course. But nothing will change how much your sister loves you." I kiss his cheek. "Let's go upstairs. I promise you will forget all about missing Avery once I have you in my bedroom."

His pensive expression transforms into a sly smile. "I finally get to see you one hundred percent naked."

"Yes." I wriggle out of his hold and trot up the steps, then pause to glance back at him over my shoulder. "What are you waiting for, Mr. Hahn?"

I remove my shoes and race into the house with Derek right behind me.

Chapter Twenty-Three

Derek

Diana pelts up the stairs while holding her dress up just enough that she won't trip over the hem, and she grins at me over her shoulder the whole time. God, I love that woman. Never thought I'd want to get into another serious relationship, but Diana proved me wrong. And now, I'm about to see her naked for the first time.

I can't wait to make love to her. But I'm only halfway up the stairs, while she's almost to the top.

When she reaches the landing, Diana stops laughing and tiptoes into her room. Pippa's room is right next door, so I'm sure Diana wants to avoid alerting the kiddo to what we're doing. Since I plan to make her scream, I think we need a slight change of venue.

I rush into Diana's room and kick the door shut. But I'm breathing too hard to speak yet, so I hold up one finger in the universal gesture for "wait a minute."

Diana does not like to wait. She tries to unzip her dress, but she can't quite reach the zipper. With a frustrated noise, she gives up and turns her back to me. "I need your assistance, please."

"Yes, ma'am," I say, though I still haven't quite caught my breath. I hurry over there and grasp the zipper on her dress, then I hesitate. Why waste an opportunity to tease her? It'll get her even hotter for me, I'm sure. So, I drag the zipper down millimeter by millimeter, and my tongue follows in its wake. Diana exhales a ragged breath. I bend my knees to keep licking a trail down her spine until the zipper reaches its end. I splay my palm over her lower back and skate it up to her shoulders, then slide it back down. "How bad do you want me now, Diana?"

"Desperately."

Rising, I glide my hands up her spine again so I can shove them under her dress and push the fabric off her shoulders. The dress falls down to the floor.

"Don't move," I say. "Don't even look back at me."

I strip off my fancy suit, tossing all the parts of it onto the bed where Diana can see it. Now that I'm naked, it's time to kick things up a notch. I move up behind her and fasten my arms around her waist, tugging her body into mine. I know she can feel my erection against her lower back, and she's breathing harder now. I paint a wet trail of kisses down her neck, while I slide one hand down until my fingers cover her mound. I wriggle my fingers to tease the hairs there, and she lets out a soft moan.

"You're so fucking sexy," I murmur into her ear. Then I plunge my fingers between her folds. "Were you ever this wet for anyone else?"

"No. Only you."

"Good." I pull my hips back just enough that I can slide my cock between her ass cheeks, and even further to feel her slick flesh on mine. "We still want to make a baby, right?"

She tips her head back, and her silky hair brushes over my chest. "Oh, yes, I still want that."

The heat of her lust excites my skin as I pump my hips slowly, and the scent of it drugs me. I glance down and see the head of my cock barely visible between her folds every time I thrust. Diana is breathing so hard that her chest heaves.

"Let's go into my room," I say. "So we won't wake up the kiddo next door."

"Yes, whatever, just fuck me."

I chuckle. "That's the plan."

Sweeping her up in my arms, I approach the adjoining door. "Can you, uh, open that for me?"

Diana stretches out one arm to grasp the knob and shove the door open.

I carry her into the other room and kick the door shut, then drop her onto the bed.

She glances at the wall behind her. "Who is on the other side of us?"

"Reese and Arden. They won't give a damn how much noise we make."

I had pulled the covers back before going downstairs for the wedding, so I don't need to do a thing to get the bed ready now. Diana rises onto her hands and knees to crawl up the bed with her hips and breasts swaying.

"You have one fine ass," I say, as I climb onto the bed where she's just rolled onto her back. "But I've got plans for other parts of your body."

I kneel over her.

She raises one leg to rub it against my dick.

A groan that's almost a growl rumbles out of me. I hook her legs over my shoulders and move forward until her knees almost touch her chest. "Damn, you're flexible. I love that."

"Yoga helps me stay limber and relaxed."

"No relaxation tonight, but your flexibility turns me on big time." I duck my head to kiss her while I ease my cock inside her inch by inch. Every time I've fucked her, she's been wet and ready for me before I even took her body. That turns me on so powerfully that I'm not sure I can hold back and take it slow. Once I'm as deep inside her as I can go, I peel my lips away from hers. "Ahhh, Diana, don't think I can wait any longer. Wanted to go slow, but—"

"Just fuck me, Derek. I don't need foreplay, and I'll go mad if you don't stop teasing me."

"Feels so good it almost hurts, doesn't it?"

She bites her lip and nods.

I feel the same way. So I plant my hands at either side of her head and start thrusting, harder and harder every time, gasping and grunting while the bed thumps and Diana cries out again. She grips my biceps and arches her neck. I punch into her faster and deeper.

"Oh God, Derek! Yes, please, yes, keep going. Never stop, never, please."

I reach down to massage her clit. My dick feels like it might explode if I don't let go and come, but I won't do that until she does. I pinch her clit—and she goes off like a supernova. Her scream would probably echo through the house, but I seal my mouth over hers to muffle it. While her body clenches my cock in pulsating waves, I throw my head back and shout as I blow apart inside her.

Sweat dribbles down my temples and onto my chest, but I keep rubbing her clit until she's done. Diana writhes and cries out, but not as loudly as she had when she first came. I slide my dick out of her sheath and thrust my fingers inside, pumping until she goes limp on the bed.

"Done, baby?" I ask, as I lie down beside her.

"Yes, I am well and truly done." She fans her face with one hand. "You are incredible, darling."

I raise my arm, and she snuggles up to me so I can hold her close. "Better do that a couple more times, just to be sure we made a baby tonight."

"Are you hoping for a boy or a girl?"

"Don't care. I'll love our kid no matter what."

She lays her palm on my chest and draws patterns on my skin with one finger. "I don't want to be a workaholic anymore. I'd like to significantly reduce my work schedule so I can spend more time with you and Pippa—and our baby. How would you feel about that?"

"That's a great idea. You've worked too hard for too long, just like Avery did. It's about time you let yourself live a little." I slip my fingers between hers, halting her finger-drawing. "I want to back off on my work too. I own the company, so I don't need to be on site every day. No more protection details for me, either. About time I delegated some of the admin tasks to my team. I'm sure Ellie, Geoffrey, Wesley, Sheldon, and the others would love to take on more responsibility."

"I'm sure you're right." She lifts her head and aims her gaze at me. "Was there no security for the wedding? I would've thought you'd want that since the bride is your sister."

"We had plenty of security. Hugh and I talked about it and decided to keep things on the down low. My team was here, but out of sight." I lift my brows. "Didn't wonder how we managed to have only two newspapers on hand to photograph the event?"

"I hadn't noticed that."

"Without my team, there would have been a lot more paparazzi."

"After tonight, what will happen if I need protection?" She drapes her leg over mine. "Close protection."

I palm her ass. "I'll always guard your body, Ms. Sangster."

"Thank you, Mr. Hahn. I feel safer already."

Someone bangs on the wall in the room next to ours. "It's our turn, mate."

"Go for it, Reese," I holler. Then I slap Diana's bottom. "Want to show them how it's done?"

"Yes, absolutely."

That's exactly what we do, and we make a lot more noise than Reese and Arden. Yeah, a bodyguard and a billionaire know how to get things done.

Chapter Twenty-Four

Diana
Seven weeks later

So much has changed in my life since the day I asked Derek to become my baby donor. These days, I can't believe I ever came up with such an idiotic plan. But if I hadn't, I might never have realized what an incredible man Derek is and how much I could love him.

I'm sitting on a chaise in the backyard of our new home, a cozy little cottage in a cozy little village. No more hustle and bustle. We like our quiet life, though we sometimes go into London for business—or pleasure. Derek and I have discovered we both love museums, though Pippa still thinks that sort of entertainment is boring. She stays overnight at Rupert's house whenever we take a trip to a museum. Pippa and Sally have become best friends.

When Hugh and Avery returned from their tropical honeymoon, they shared some news with us first. They're going to have a baby in slightly less than seven months. Derek and I were both thrilled by their announcement, and I know Derek especially looks forward to becoming an uncle.

Today, I have news of my own.

I wait until Pippa goes into the house to use the loo, then I walk over to the barbecue grill where Derek is flipping hamburgers. "Could you take a break for a moment?"

"Sure. These burgers need a few more minutes." He steps away from the grill. "What's up?"

I've never been one to procrastinate, so I blurt out, "The stick turned blue."

"What stick?"

"The one I'm going to shove up your arse. What do you think? I took a home pregnancy test."

"Ohhh, that kind of stick." His expression goes blank. "Are you saying…"

"I'm pregnant. I'll need to see a doctor to confirm it, just to be sure."

He sweeps me up in his arms and twirls us round and round while grinning and whooping.

"What's going on?" Pippa asks.

I can just barely see her standing on the patio. The world has become a blur. I start laughing too, even while I say, "Set me down, please, Derek."

He sets me on the ground. "Did you tell Pippa yet?"

"No, of course not."

"What didn't you tell me?" Pippa asks, as she approaches us.

"Diana is pregnant," Derek says, while still grinning. "You're about to have a cousin."

Pippa shrieks and jumps up and down, clapping furiously. "That's brilliant, Mum! I can't wait."

I can't help smiling. "Technically, our child will be Pippa's brother or sister, since I adopted her."

"Who cares about the technicalities?" Derek says. "We've got everything we ever wanted."

He's spot on, of course. Just a few months ago, I would have never thought I'd find this kind of happiness. Pippa brought me so much joy, but deep down, I'd always wanted more. I wanted a family, and now I have one. Hugh and Avery are part of our family too, and vice versa.

Derek clears his throat. "I, uh, was going to wait until dessert before I did this. But now seems like the perfect time." He drops to one knee in front of me. After digging about in his trouser pocket for a moment, he pulls out a small satin box and holds it up to me. Derek flips the lid open. "Diana, will you marry me?"

"Yes, love, of course I will."

He slips the ring onto my finger, then leaps up to pull me into his arms and kiss me.

And Pippa shrieks again.

When Derek relinquishes my lips, he wears a sheepish expression. "I should've done this a lot sooner. I wanted to ask you the day after Avery and Hugh's wedding, but it didn't seem right to horn in on their big moment. Then we started house hunting, and after that we needed to furnish the place…"

I seal his lips with my fingers. "You don't need to apologize. I know how hectic these past few months have been. This was the perfect time to pop that question."

Pippa is grinning at us. "How should we celebrate?"

Derek's lips curve into a sly smile. "How else? With a big, huge, gigantic party. We'll invite everybody—Brits, Scots, Americans, and whoever else. That might mean we'll need to commandeer Sommerleigh House for the occasion."

"Avery and Hugh won't mind at all."

Pippa runs over to hug both me and Derek at the same time. "This is the best thing that's ever happened in the history of the world."

I laugh. "That might be a slight exaggeration. But you should go grab my mobile so we can call Avery to let her know. She'll want to help organize the big do."

Pippa races into the house.

And I wrap my arms around Derek's neck, tickling his nape with my fingertips. "On a scale of one to ten, how happy are you today?"

"One million. How about you?"

"At least a billion."

He bumps his nose into mine. "Well, that's appropriate for a billionaire like you. Can I up my estimate to two billion?"

"Let's call it an even ten billion for both of us."

"It's a deal."

Precisely three weeks later, our little family arrives at Sommerleigh for the big do. But "big" hardly describes what Avery and the American Wives Club have created for us. They've turned the garden and lawn into a magical fairyland, with sparkling white lights and flower garlands draped over every bush, table, and chair, not to mention the house itself. Inside the manor, even more garlands decorate the staircase and every room in the house.

Yes, those women have gone overboard. But I don't care. It's the loveliest thing anyone has ever done for me, and I know Pippa and Derek feel the same way.

I glance down at my engagement ring, and a wonderfully warm glow blossoms in my chest. For too long, I'd let my past taint my present and my future. All it took was for one stubborn, sexy, incredible man to shatter all the walls I'd built around myself. Avery and Hugh also played a vital role in my transformation from uptight workaholic to a happy, settled woman with a family and more mates than I could ever hope to have found.

Avery rushes up to me and drags me into a boisterous hug. "Oh, Diana, isn't it wonderful? We're both having babies, and we'll be sisters soon."

Tears sting my eyes, but they're a sign of happiness, and I am not ashamed to show my feelings anymore. "Yes, darling, it is wonderful. But you are already my sister—in my heart, if not officially yet."

Avery releases me and holds up my hand to study my ring. "Derek knows how to pick jewelry. It's the perfect size and style for you."

Yes, that man always knows precisely what I need and want.

I lay my arm across Avery's shoulders and lead her toward the garden. "Now, dear, you need to explain to me what the American Wives Club, British Branch, actually is."

"Well, you're British, like Alex. So we created a special offshoot of the Club for people like you guys. Derek will become an honorary member. I'll explain it more later."

I stop us beside a rhododendron that now wears garlands of various types. "I know I didn't appreciate it at the time, but I'm glad you meddled in my life. You are an angel, Avery. If I hadn't met you, I might never have found Derek and realized I want more out of life than work."

"Hugh thought you might never forgive us for interfering. But even my hubby is getting in the meddling spirit these days."

"Do you lot have your sights set on another bloke or lady who needs help?"

"What do you think?" Avery wags her eyebrows, then whispers, "Would you like to help us out with our next project?"

"Perhaps I will. Who is your next project?"

She glances around as if she's making sure no one will overhear us. "Dominic Rigby and Chelsea Vance."

"Oh, yes, dear. Count me in."

Want more of Dominic and Chelsea? Experience their story in *One Hot Favor* (Hot Brits, Book Nine).

Love the

Hot Brits

series?

Visit
AnnaDurand.com

to subscribe to her newsletter
for updates on forthcoming books in this series
&
to receive free gifts for signing up!

Anna Durand is a bestselling, multi-award-winning author of contemporary and paranormal romance. Her books have earned bestseller status on every major retailer and wonderful reviews from readers around the world. But that's the boring spiel. Here are the really cool things you want to know about Anna!

Born on Lackland Air Force Base in Texas, Anna grew up moving here, there, and everywhere thanks to her dad's job as an instructor pilot. She's lived in Texas (twice), Mississippi, California (twice), Michigan (twice), and Alaska—and now Ohio.

As for her writing, Anna has always made up stories in her head, but she didn't write them down until her teen years. Those first awful books went into the trash can a few years later, though she learned a lot from those stories. Eventually, she would pen her first romance novel, the paranormal romance *Willpower*, and she's never looked back since.

Want even more details about Anna? Get access to her extended bio when you subscribe to her newsletter and download the free bonus ebook, *Hot Scots Confidential*. You'll also get hot deleted scenes, character interviews, fun facts, and more! Plus you'll receive the short story *Tempted by a Kiss* and mutliple bonus chapters in both ebook and audiobook formats.

Visit AnnaDurand.com to sign up.